True Control 4.2

Books by Willow Madison

True Nature

True Beginnings

True Choices

True Control 4.1

we were one once 1

we were one once 2

Existential Angst

the SAYER

True Control 4.2

Willow Madison

Madison, Willow

True Control (True Series, Book Four . Two)

Front Cover Design by David Colon (www.colonfilm.com); Back Cover Design by XIX (www.thenineteen.net)

This is a work of fiction. Names, characters, places and incidents are either the product of the author's imagination or are used fictitiously, and any resemblance to actual persons, living or dead, business establishments, events or locales is entirely coincidental.

This book is intended for adults only. Spanking and other sexual activities represented in this book are fantasies only, intended for adults. Nothing in the book should be interpreted as advocating any non-consensual spanking activity or the spanking of minors.

www.willowmadisonbooks.com

ISBN-13: 978-0-9963191-5-7
ISBN-10: 0-9963191-5-8

1 Him

"Did you find her?" My brother is in the hallway before I can even open the door all the way.

I only shake my head at Jake. I'm too shocked, too numb to trust speaking right now. I feel hot tears in my throat, behind my eyes. I blink and try to breathe. *This can't be happening.*

I hear Jeff talking behind me, but everything sounds far away right now. I move further into my living room, but don't sit. Just look around. It was only a few hours ago I came home and found Lucy gone.

"I called a friend at the Missing Persons Unit. He's going to come over. We found Lucy's purse and cell phone in the garbage near her doctor's office. He's checking on this first." Jeff fills in what little we do know.

"Can't the police look for her now?" Jake puts words to my own anger.

"She's an adult. Unless there's reason to believe something happened to her..." Jeff is frustrated too. I can tell he's barely holding his own temper in check. I almost hit him when he told me we just have to wait here for his friend to show up. I blame myself for not having him drive Lucy this afternoon. *If only...*

"Obviously something happened! She wouldn't just disappear like this." *My thoughts exactly.* But on the ride back here, Jeff explained how the police operate when something like this happens. It's going to take all my influence to get any sort of investigation going quickly.

"I called an investigator we use at the firm. I'm not waiting for the police to start looking for Lucy, Jake." I pat him on his shoulder and move into the kitchen. He nods his head and takes a seat at the table. I come back with three glasses and a bottle of scotch. I don't sit, but Jeff does.

We drink quietly, each staring at nothing.

I keep thinking about lunch today. *The last time I saw Lucy.* She wasn't feeling well. I'd hoped it was morning sickness. *We've only been trying a few months now, but it could've been.*

Jake picks up the list of chores I left on the table for Lucy this morning. She didn't get to many of them. I'd warned her when I left after lunch to get everything done before we had to leave for the concert tonight or she'd have a hard time sitting through it. I smile thinking of this. *I wish I could go back in time.*

Jake's voice interrupts my thoughts, "She was having a hard time with this, ya know?"

I frown, "What?"

"With your lists. Your demands. She was having a hard time adjusting." Jake puts the list back down and takes another sip.

I only stare in disbelief at him. *Where does he get off telling me what Lucy thought about anything*? "What makes you say that?"

"She told me." His jaw is set, but his eyes look…*what? Guilty?*

"Lucy told you that? When?"

Jake takes a deep breath and puts his glass down. He sits back and faces me fully. "Today. This morning, when I saw her."

I only blink for a second. Jeff reacts though, the ex-cop in him quick with questions. "*You* saw Lucy today? Where?"

Jake doesn't take his eyes off of me, but he answers Jeff in a calm voice, "Here. Around 10:30."

"You came *here* to see me?" I'm leaning against the wall now, just staring at my brother. He knows I wouldn't have been here. He knows that our firm has a set office meeting every Friday. Dad doesn't let anyone skip it.

"No. To see Lucy." I'm not surprised by his answer. But I am pissed.

I move to stand over him. Jeff gets up and tries to stand between us a little. But Jake just stays in the same spot, with the same calm look and voice. "Why would you come here to see Lucy, Jake? What about?"

"I check up on her. See how she's doing…"

I laugh, one harsh grunt really. "Why would you do that, little brother?"

Jake is still calm, but his jaw clenches again and he reaches for the scotch. His hand is white, squeezing around the glass, a mirror to my own. "Because I care about Lucy. She's my sister after all." His grin almost gets him knocked out. Jeff grabs my arm as I twitch with the desire to hit Jake. I want to hit something in my anger and frustration. *Sitting here, talking about Lucy, while she's God knows where!*

Jake pours more scotch for himself, no longer looking at me.

I shake Jeff's hand off my arm and turn to sit on the sofa. He sits back down next to Jake, still between us though.

Jake speaks up again, "You may as well know, Max. I've been seeing Lucy every Friday…since that night we picked her up at that Italian place…" He knows he can speak freely in front of Jeff. But he's not saying that was the night I beat Lucy pretty badly for letting another man touch her while she was out with her friends.

"So you've been coming to *my* house, to see *my* wife…for five fucking months, behind my back?!" *I can't believe what I'm hearing.*

"Yes."

I can see Jeff tense, ready to jump up if I do. I take a breath and a sip. *I need to stay calm. Police may be knocking on the door any second. Hell, Lucy could come walking through the door any second. I'll have plenty of time to sort out what all this means then.*

I need to think through anything that I do right now. *Punching my brother would not be a good move. But it would feel good.* I grin at this thought.

Jake frowns at the change in my look. I sit back. "So what did you and Lucy do on your little visits?"

"Talked."

"About what?"

"You mostly. Your marriage. Your demands." Jake sounds angry again.

"I see. And you think…what? I was too hard on her and that's why she's gone?"

"Maybe." He takes a big drink, glancing at Jeff. "I *know* you were too hard on her. Especially that night."

"That's not your call to make." We've had this conversation before. He never said anything about talking to Lucy, but Jake's tried to get me to ease up on her a few times.

"I saw her two days later, Max. She could hardly move. She couldn't sit." His voice rises with anger, but I don't react.

"She got what she deserved."

"She wouldn't tell me what you did to her…wouldn't let me see. But she didn't deserve *that*!"

"Again…not your call, Jake. She's *my* wife. *My* property."

"Do you hear yourself? She's your wife…that doesn't give you the right to *hurt* her like that."

"Yes. It does." I can tell that Jake wants to hit me. His hands keep clenching and unclenching on his knees. *He thinks we're so different. I know we're not.* "I saw how you looked at her that night, Jake. You think you would've done any different?"

It's like I slapped him. "I…I wouldn't have hurt her like that…"

"No? You looked pretty pissed off too…another man touching Lucy…" He tries to put his face back to neutral, but I see that I've touched a nerve. "You think I haven't noticed the way you look at her? The way you always find a reason to be near her? You think I'm stupid, little brother?" He only shakes his head. "You think you would've just gone home that night…and what? Had a nice chat with Lucy about her behavior? You would've only scolded her for acting like a whore?"

"She's not a whore."

"No. And she'll never act like one again either." *This feels good. Talking about Lucy.* My *Lucy. I can almost imagine that she's in the bedroom crying after a good beating for whatever she's been up to today.* "You would've done exactly the same as I did. You would've punished her." He shakes his head again. "That night, you would've taken a belt to her too." He still only shakes his head, but I see the doubt in his eyes. *He wants to think he's so far removed from how Dad raised us. That he's not just like me, just like Dad. He is.*

"You won't be coming here again. You won't be seeing Lucy alone ever again. You understand me?" He doesn't answer. Just clenches his jaw. "Answer me, boy?"

He laughs. My same harsh grunt. "You're not Dad, Max. I don't *have* to do what you say."

I jump up. Jake jumps up. Jeff jumps up. I've never been so close to hitting my brother. I can't stop seeing red and wanting to beat him. "Go. Get out before I do something…I don't want to do."

I've always protected Jake. Watched over him as kids, took his beatings from Mom when I could. Tried to do the same with Ron in the beginning. I never imagined a time when I would be the one who wanted to hit him. *I was wrong.*

He interfered with my marriage. He messed up. And I can't stand the sight of him in my home. Not now. With Lucy missing.

2 Her

*The floor is starting to hurt my butt. I think this is the…seventeenth time I've said this to myself in the last…*glance at my watch…*hour.*

Oh God. It's been hours since I left the house. Since I threw my phone and purse away. *Where are you?! Please get home…*

I'm in so much trouble. I'm in so much trouble. And that would be the hundredth time…thousandth time?…I've had that thought.

I messed up. And now I'm trapped. I haven't cursed in so long, but I take a deep breath and whisper to myself, "Shit." *That felt good. Wanna go for broke?* "SHIT!" I giggle loudly.

"Lucy?!" *Oh thank God!*

"Jake? I'm up here!" I wrap my hands around the multiple metal bands and shake the cage. I can hear him running up the stairs. He's out of breath by the time he gets to the top floor. The look on Jake's face is so funny, I giggle despite everything.

"What the hell are you doing here?" He looks at the elevator doors and me like he doesn't recognize either one.

"I came here to see you...to talk to you." I pull my hands back from the bars. "I got stuck."

"No shit. The elevator hasn't worked for more than two seconds for the last month." He tries to pull the cage door open but it won't budge. The elevator made it almost to the top and then stopped about a foot too low. The door opened, but the old inner cage door wouldn't.

"I know that now..."

"Try pressing the button up."

I glare at him, "Tried that about five hundred times already. I've pressed every button." But I grin. Now that he's here, I feel better. Calmer. *He'll help me to figure out what to do just as soon as he gets me out of here.* "The alarm doesn't work either, by the way."

He shakes his head. "Hang on. Let me see what I have that might work." He walks away and opens the door to his apartment.

Jake bought this warehouse building a few months ago. He plans to make the two bottom floors his new architectural offices, rent the third floor and have the top floor as his new home. Eventually. Right now, the only floor somewhat useable is this top floor of semi-converted loft space. I was able to get in because I knew he used his birthday as the code for the door. I didn't know that I'd be stuck in here all afternoon waiting for him.

Oh God. I'm in so much trouble.

Jake returns with a crowbar and a giant wrench looking thing. "Stand back." I move to the corner. He shoves the crowbar into the small space between the cage and the edge of the elevator frame. Watching him strain and work, I'm reminded how much he looks like Max. Same gorgeous green eyes and strong muscles.

The metal groans; Jake groans, teeth gritting with effort. Finally, the cage door grinds and scrapes open a little, then springs open further. Jake almost falls back with the release of pressure on the crowbar. I jump up and out with Jake grabbing me in his arms.

"I can't believe you're here. You're safe." He doesn't let go. I can feel his heart beating hard under his light jacket.

"Of course I'm safe, silly."

His look changes quickly into the stern, angry look I'm used to seeing from Max. I've only seen this a few times on Jake. I shrink as his hands grip my arms tighter. He shakes me with each word, "What were you thinking? Coming here?"

"I needed to see you again…"

"Max is worried sick looking for you." *Oh God, please don't remind me.* His look darkens even more. "He has the police coming to your house right now, Lucy."

"Oh, God."

"Yeah…Oh, God, is right. Get in here." He pulls me into his apartment and slams the door behind us. "Explain yourself." *How like Max he sounds.*

I haven't been in his apartment since the first weekend he moved in. He threw a small housewarming party for himself. I met his friends and staff. Max and I stayed to help him clean up. I smile remembering how drunk they both were, laughing like kids late into the night.

Looking around, he's done a lot with the big open space since then. A lot of new furniture and walls. It's almost a home now.

I turn to look at him and I'm shocked at how angry he is. The Traeger men have a special look when they get angry. It's a deep, thoughtful, brooding frown, with eyes shaded, jaw clenched, shoulders rounded like cats ready to spring, whole body tense. I've only seen it on Jake once. I shudder the way I always do when I see Max this way.

"I said, explain yourself, girl."

"You said this morning that you were coming home after lunch. To work on this place." He only nods, look unchanged. "So...so I came here to see you." I swallow. "I skipped my doctor's appointment. I rang from downstairs, but figured either the buzzer didn't work or you were up here making too much noise to hear me, so I let myself in."

"You shouldn't be here…" But he stops himself, running his long fingers through his dark waves. He breathes out heavily, but the look only softens a little. "I'm going to have to call Max." He turns to get his cell phone out of his bag, on the counter where he left it.

"Wait! Please…"

He stops, but doesn't turn around. "What happened today? With your purse and phone? Max said he found it in a garbage bin?" He finally does turn around again to look at me. I shudder once more at the anger I see.

3 Him

Jeff is still on the phone with his friend, Detective Killaney. He told me in between answering and asking questions that Killaney has bagged the purse and phone and will take it to the station before coming here. *Good. It's a start at least.*

My investigator already said that the cab driver who dropped Lucy off near her doctor's office didn't have any information. Neither did the security guard at the front desk of the office building.

I walk into our bedroom. I've left everything just the way it was when I got home earlier. Jeff said not to touch anything unnecessarily. But I walk into the closet. *No dry cleaning.* Lucy didn't even finish this chore. She probably intended to pick up my suit for tonight on her way home from the doctor.

Fuck. My Lucy. Lost. I can't take this.

This feeling of helplessness. Powerlessness. *I've never known this feeling.*

Even when I was a kid and Mom was at her worst…I always felt like I had some control over my life. I was a tough kid. I stayed because of Jake…hell, even because of Mom. She needed me, to take care of her. Until Ron came along.

He took care of all of us.

I pick up my cell and dial his number. Dad may be needed to get any investigation fast tracked. I'm sick waiting for him to pick up though. *How do I tell the man who taught me everything I know about being a man, taking control, staying in control…that I've completely lost it?*

Fuck.

4 Her

Uh oh. Max went downtown looking for me? I am in more trouble than I thought... "I threw it away."

Jake blinks and raises his eyebrows with a grunted laugh. "Why would you do something so stupid?"

I get defensive at this. "Because I know Max tracks my phone!"

"So what?"

"So he'd know that I came *here*..." *Now who's being stupid?*

Jake rubs his chin. It's a move I've seen him do whenever he's thinking, but doesn't want to say what. "Just say it."

"What?" He frowns at me, his look still a blend of irritation and anger.

"You have something on your mind…just say it."

He drops his hands, "What are you doing here, Lucy?"

I swallow. It was hours ago when I came to talk to him. I realized what a bad move it was after the first half hour stuck in the elevator. *I've made a big mess today. And I can't see any way out of it now.*

I didn't really think it through. I didn't give myself a chance to think. I impulsively threw my purse and phone away right in front of Dr. Patel's building. And then I walked quickly away. No cab. No bus. I walked to Jake's. That was almost ten blocks. My feet were killing me in the little sandals I'm wearing. My legs were cold in the dress against the early spring wind.

And then getting here. No Jake. And an elevator that acted like a prison.

Yeah…pretty stupid.

I put my hands over my face and let out a little cry. *I'm scared now.*

Jake wraps me in his arms, holding my head and shoulders with his strong hands. He held me like this that first time he came to see me on that Friday. *That seems like so long ago.*

But I've thought about it often. That Wednesday night with Max. That Friday with Jake.

I shake with tears in his arms.

5 Him

"Yes, Sir. I'll let you know as soon as the detective gets here." I listen a little more as Dad assures me that he'll be making calls on his way to my place in the meantime. "Yeah. That's a good idea to leave Mom at home for now. It might be a zoo here soon."

I put my cell in my pocket after looking to see if I missed any calls or texts. *Maybe Lucy is with her friend Laura after all? Or in the hospital.* My investigators are checking this next.

Please...don't let her be hurt...

I don't know what I'd do if anything happened to Lucy...she's my life. My everything. She has been since the first time I saw her.

Just before our wedding, waiting for the door to open, waiting to see her for the first time that day...this is how I felt.

This separation. The need to see her again. To see her smile, her eyes. She has my heart and it feels like it's tearing in my chest right now.

I want to punch something. I need to be doing something!

I walk into the living room again. Jeff is waiting at the table. He stands when I walk in. "Jeff...give me something...tell me your friend is doing something right now to find her..."

"Tom is doing everything he can. Until this is an official investigation and he's assigned, he can only do so much..." *Not what I needed to hear.* I growl and turn around in a small circle slowly. *Fuck!*

"Dad's on his way here. He's going to see what he can do to speed up that official assignment anyway." I reach for the bottle of scotch and notice Jeff watching me. I don't give a shit. I need a drink right now. Or I need to punch something. He seems to get it and backs off with his hands up in the air.

I walk out into the night air with my glass. *My Lucy. Somewhere out here...Where are you, little girl?*

6 Her

I get control over my tears slowly. Jake keeps his hands pressed on my head and shoulder though. His fingers rub my curls and the skin on my neck. I start to feel uncomfortable and push slightly against him.

He lets go, almost pushing me away.

"I'm sorry… I'm just scared. You said Max was looking for me?"

He nods, "Yeah. He went downtown with Jeff. Even called me to keep a look out for you at your place." He reacts to my look. "Sit down." I let him lead me to his sofa. He sits close to me, keeping his hand on mine. His other hand pushes my hair back, rubbing my arm.

I like his touch, it's gentle. I need a reminder that Max can be gentle too, like his brother. "I…I wasn't thinking..." tears well up again, but I don't stop, I just let them fall onto our hands in my lap, without blinking. "I dropped my purse and phone, thinking I'd tell Max that I was mugged…" I look up into Jake's emerald green eyes. They're not soft, but his face is, "Remember when we were mugged in the park?" He nods.

"I figured that would be okay. He'd forgive me for missing my appointment. And it was an excuse why he couldn't reach me, just in case. But…But you weren't home." I sob again. I can't help it. I'm in a desperate spot and I know it. *I can't explain away this amount of time…my phone and purse…Oh, God…he called the police! I'm not a good liar…I don't know how I thought I could make this work!*

Shit. And I feel the familiar twinge of guilt at disobeying Max's rule about cussing, even in my own head. I cry louder.

Jake pulls me into a hug again. His embrace feels good. It shouldn't, but it does.

7 Him

I walk back inside, hanging up the phone. "Your friend's here. He's coming up." Jeff only nods and heads towards the door to open it. I set my empty glass down on the table and take a seat.

I've had clients that have had run-ins with the police before. Kids in trouble. High-profile wife in an accident injuring someone. A few civil lawsuits that started with criminal investigations. But I've never had the need to call a cop myself.

I don't really know what to expect. Until Killaney walks in. And he's exactly what I would picture. Ill-fitting suit, short, sloppy, red-faced. Alert. His eyes take everything in before focusing on me. His hand is extended before his bag is even on the table.

"Mr. Traeger. I'm sorry to meet under these circumstances." I only mumble a hello and shake his hand.

"Jeff has shared some good stories about working with you over a beer or two." He's eyeing my glass and the bottle of scotch.

"Can I get you a drink, Detective?"

He licks his lips. "Well…technically, I'm not on the job right now…so, sure." I don't have to ask if he wants any scotch; it's obvious. *Not off to a good start*, but I nod to Jeff to get another glass.

"So what did you find out so far?"

"Not much unfortunately." He lifts his glass in cheers before taking a big drink. "I have the purse and phone bagged and we'll hopefully pull prints pretty quick. But it looks like a simple robbery if anything. No cash, but cards were all left. Strange that the perp wouldn't take the phone, but it's not the latest model maybe…"

I nod. I'd already checked online for any charges to the cards. Nothing new.

"Do you have any ideas for where Lucy would be?" I only shake my head. "No friend or family she might be staying with…?"

I shake my head again, "No. I've already called everyone around here. Her brother and best friend. No one's seen or talked to her today." I stop, thinking, except *my* brother.

"Hmm…and you think they'd tell you if she was with them…?"

I don't like where he's going with this. "Yes, Detective."

"I gotta ask, Max." He takes another big drink. "Usually, in these cases, the wife will show up on her own. Usually turns out to be just a marital spat…" I don't say anything. "Did you have a fight with your wife, Max?"

8 Her

Jake finally pulls me away again. He gets up and grabs a few napkins for me. "Blow your nose, Rudolph." I laugh at this. I know my face gets all red and blotchy when I cry. *Max says I'm beautiful like this...when he makes me cry anyway.* I try to hold my breath to stop from hiccupping, but it's too late.

Jake laughs at me and grabs two bottles of water for us too. But he doesn't sit back down next to me, just keeps watching me as I drink almost half the bottle in one long gulp. "Thank you."

"So what did you need to talk to me about so urgently that you made such a fuck-up move today?" He's angry again. His voice has that edge again and it's not like him to curse at me.

Once more, I'm feeling defensive. "What you said this morning. We didn't get to...to finish talking about what would

happen. You left because Max would be home any minute…
But I needed to know what you meant."

He rubs his chin again before running his hand through
his hair. He glares at me. "I had to tell Max about seeing you
today." He watches as the blood runs out of my face. *Trouble
just keeps piling up for me.* "Yeah…he was pretty pissed about
it." He moves around so he's standing right in front of me. I
look up at him, through my lashes. He's giving me a pretty
good preview of the look I'll see on Max's face. He cups my
chin with his fingers and lifts my face to him more. But he
only gives me that strange look of his, like he's looking
through me, looking for something. He drops his hand and sits
on the coffee table, facing me.

I lower my chin and eyes. I know what I'm going to say
will only make him angrier. "I needed to know what your
mom said to you. Why you were taking back everything that
you said before."

"That's why you blew off your doctor's? Why you came
here and didn't tell anyone?" I don't need to look up to know
that he's glaring at me. I only nod. "Goddammit, Lucy!" He
jumps up and heads into the kitchen.

I watch as he opens a bottle of beer from his fridge and
takes a deep drink. He keeps watching me, slowing returning
to sit on the coffee table again. He still has that deep frown
look. I slide back a little in the sofa, away from him.

He wipes his lips and takes a deep breath. "I wasn't
taking everything back. I meant what I said before too. I do
think Max is too hard on you." I can finally look at him again.
Jake is only a little softer, though. "My conversation with
Mom…" He sighs. "She said she knew that I struggled more

than Max with how Dad was. But she hoped that I'd figure it out for myself. That tough love is still love. That's how she put it. The man would slap her right in front of us, and she loved him. He'd treat her like a child, sending her to their room…everything he did." He stops and looks knowingly at me. "But she loved him. She said she's grateful that he came along. That she never knew what love and security was before him."

"And that made you…what, rethink things?" I'm still trying to figure out what he meant this morning.

He shakes his head. "No. She did admit to all the abuse Max told you about…I even remembered a little hearing her talk…" His voice cracks at this admission. He's never really wanted to remember anything. Max was always frustrated about this. He said Jake needed to remember to understand that things were better with Ron than without him. But Jake was too young to remember much of anything from their earliest childhood.

"Mom apologized to me. Said that without Dad she doesn't know what she would've done…to us, to herself. That she was suicidal back then. Depressed. On and off using drugs and men to forget about the two boys she had at home who needed her." He looks at me with watery eyes. I lean forward and put my hands over his on his knees.

"That's how she put it. She didn't hold anything back…maybe because I waited so long to talk to her." He takes a deep breath. "But she told me that I need to stop blaming Dad. That she chose to stay. She chose to live by his rules, his discipline. That she's never regretted the life she has with him. And he's never really hurt her…not really. Just like he never really hurt us. And I know this much is true…I'm a stronger person because of Dad. Because of the love I had from Mom."

I only nod again. I don't know what to say. *This is what I came here to find out, but…I don't know what to think of it.* Jake's always struggled with his upbringing. It's why I talked to him that Friday. It's why I've confided in him. Because he shares my questions and gives me insights into Max, how they were both raised.

"She also told me…" He stops. His face turns from sad to stern to that odd look again so quickly; I imagine this is what Max sees when he says I'm so expressive. "She told me that I need to stop thinking that I can protect you."

I frown. "Why would she say that?"

"Because she knows that I care about you… And I talked to her about you once."

"You did?" He never told me this. I'm not sure how this makes me feel. *Uncomfortable I guess is the easiest way to put it.*

"Yeah. It was just before I bought this place." He looks around. I know he was proud of himself for getting this building on his own, for deciding to make such a big move for himself and his business. He really wants to showcase his work here. I look around too. There's only one light on in the kitchen, but I can see that it's looking nice so far.

"I told her I always thought I'd wait until I had a wife by my side." He was looking over my head, but he lowers his eyes to lock with mine. Definitely uncomfortable, but I can't look away. "I told her that I didn't think it was right, how Max won't let you make any decisions for yourself. That he doesn't appreciate having a good wife like you."

I swallow. "What…what did your mom say?"

"She told me that Max's marriage was none of my business. And that I shouldn't be thinking so much about my brother's wife."

I can't think clearly. He's too close. The room is too dark. I swallow again. But Jake doesn't move away. I watch as he squeezes my hands still on his knees. I don't lift my eyes from his fingers, but I can see his look getting sterner again. "Lucy, you came here to talk to me…and I'm glad you did. You've made a royal mess of everything, but it gives me a chance," I can hear his frown, "Look at me, girl." Obedient puppy, I lift my eyes and chin. "It gives me a chance to set things straight with you." I can only swallow again and nod slightly.

9 Him

"Lucy and I don't fight." I pour myself a little more scotch and tilt the bottle towards Killaney, he nods. I pour a little more for him too.

"Never? Wow. You're a lucky man. My wife and me…we're like cats and dogs thrown into a wet sack together most days." He takes a big gulp. "Having three boys in only four years doesn't help much." He laughs. "You got any kids?"

"No. We've only been married six months." *I don't want to discuss this.*

"Newlyweds…that's nice." He looks at his glass, making the scotch leg's wrap around the inside before tilting it up again for big drink. "So what's with the list?"

He means the list of chores for Lucy of course. It's still sitting on the table. "Chores for my wife. She didn't get to most of them today."

He takes out a small notepad and pen from his pocket. He pulls the list closer to his seat with the pen, but doesn't pick it up. "This your handwriting or hers?"

"Mine."

"You always leave her a list of chores?"

"Yes."

"And she doesn't argue…you two don't fight?" He's laughing, looking at me with just his eyes raised from the list.

"No. Lucy's a good girl. She does as she's told."

"Wow. I guess that makes you a *very* lucky man, Max." *The conversation is starting to shift. I'd like to keep it on track.* I glance at Jeff, but he's staying out of it, hanging back on the sofa.

"So what is the next step in finding Lucy?"

10 Her

"Lucy, I've appreciated these past months." I can feel Jake's warm fingers on mine. "But I don't think that Max is going to allow it to continue and…" He swallows, pulling his hands back. I pull mine back too. I can't stop staring into his eyes. He hasn't hardly blinked even. "Well…I'm not sure it was a good idea for either of us anyway."

I reach and put just my fingertips over his hand. "It helped me a lot, Jake…being able to talk to you. It did help."

He smiles, but it doesn't reach his eyes. They stay stern, even getting a little angrier with me again. "That's just it. You wouldn't be here now if it had helped." He shakes his head, runs his fingers through his hair again…his frustrated move. "I meant it this morning. I've been wrong. About everything. About you. About Max."

"That's why I came. I needed to know what you meant…but you just left so quickly…"

"I left because I didn't want to cause any problems for you…for Max. I was going to tell you that I wasn't going to be coming over anymore. That it wasn't a good idea and if Max ever knew…" He doesn't need to finish this thought. I shiver a little thinking about what's waiting for me.

He grins, seeing my fear. "Yeah. He'll go apeshit after this." He tilts his head back and stares at his ceiling for a moment. "I was wrong to interfere. I was wrong to check on you that first time and to keep coming back."

"But I liked our friendship. I liked that I could talk to you. You helped me to see things from Max's side…" My voice is small. I don't want to lose the one person I can talk to besides Max… *even more than Max in some ways.*

He glares at me. I back away again, startled by the intensity of his anger so quickly flared. "And I *liked* seeing you. A lot. You want the truth?" I don't move.

He gets up and walks a few feet away before turning on me again. "You are such a stupid little girl, Lucy! You have no idea…" But he doesn't finish.

I stand slowly, "Maybe I should go…" I turn to leave.

He grabs my arm and yanks me back to sitting on the sofa. I'm shocked. He's never touched me so roughly before. He's reminded me of Max so often in the past months, but never quite like this. I'm almost afraid of him.

He shakes his head and clenches his fists for a moment before walking away. I don't get up again, just watch him go back to the beer on the counter and finish it in one long drink, staring at me. When he comes back, it's with that same rolled shoulder, deep look. I sit back on the sofa more again.

He sits back down on the coffee table, our knees touching.

"That night. The night Max and I picked you up and we saw that guy with his hand on you." My cheeks flare thinking of how angry Max was. What he did to me. But I remember that Jake shared his brother's anger that night too. Even that Friday when he came over, he was still angry. Even when he held me.

He puts his hands on my knees. They're almost hot against me now. "Max was right. He said it today to me, when I told him that I started seeing you ever since that night."

"He was right about what?" I don't want to know, but I can't stop meeting Jake's stare, I can't help asking.

"That we're not so different." He squeezes my knees, not a tickle, but a firm grip. Like his grip on my arm, not a touch I'm used to, from him at least. "Maybe if I'd been more honest with myself…I could've been more honest with you…" He doesn't let go and I don't move. "I could've told you what a bad idea it was for us to meet behind Max's back. I could've told you not to trust me. I could've told you…" He stops though, breaking the spell by letting go of my legs and sitting back.

I swallow hard, *this was not how today was supposed to go. I didn't think it through, but I imagined talking to Jake, feeling better about finding out if I'm pregnant, feeling stronger about talking to Max about my fears tonight. Not sitting here with a mess at home and a mess here. I've made a mess of everything.*

"Jake…I came here because you're my friend. Because I needed to hear what you had to say. Because hearing you say that…that you'd changed your mind…that I should stop questioning everything and just be what Max wants…" I can feel tears in my eyes again. Ever since that Friday, since Max showed his true brutal anger to me…I've questioned if I can stay. If I can be the wife that he needs, submit to his level of painful punishments…raise a child the way he wants. Jake knew this. To hear him say today that I should just stop thinking and be with Max…*Today, when I might find out that I'm pregnant already…I needed to talk to him. But not like this.*

I didn't think it was possible, but his look darkens even more. He leans in a little and I lean back a lot. "Friends? You think I've been your friend these months, Lucy?" I nod. He laughs, a rattled painful sound in his throat. "You want to talk about Max. Then talk to *him*, Lucy! Me? I can tell you how *I* feel if you'd like to know."

He grins, a dark twist to his normally sweet smile. "I've lied to myself. To you. All my life, I've tried to deny how I feel. What makes me tick…in bed, in life. With women. I've tried to toe a different line than the one Ron wanted. I tried to pretend that treating women as equals, partners…that that is the way it should be. That all I wanted was a woman I could have by my side, sharing in all my successes and hers."

He gets up and opens another beer. He takes a small drink and slams it down. I jump at the sound and splash on the counter. "I've fucking lied to myself!" He comes back to stand over me. And I try to stand up. "Sit." I truly feel like a puppy now. I try to look calm, crossing my legs and pulling my dress down over my knee. But I don't say anything, too afraid that anything I'd say would only set him off more. I'm in uncharted territory here with Jake.

"I wanted to believe that if…that if you were *my* wife, I'd treat you better. That's what I've been doing these past months…convincing myself that I'm better than my brother. That I'd control my anger with you better. That I'd respect you more. That I'd make you happier." He's panting with the effort to control his breathing, his fists clenched, his face red with anger, his voice loud with it.

"Oh." It's not really a word, more the wind knocked out of me. *I* have *been stupid. I had no idea he felt this way about me.*

11 Him

"The next step is convincing the powers that be that she hasn't run off. That something happened to her." Killaney puts up his hand before I can say anything to this. "I know you've told me about tracking her phone and messages. You've talked to her friends and family. You don't believe that she could be out just having fun…maybe getting back at you, wanting to make you worry or something?"

"No. Lucy would know better than to make me worry."

He's appraising me again, his eyes taking in how angry his words are making me. The thought that Lucy could be hurt is more than I can think, that someone has her, that someone took her from me. *But the thought that she's gone on her own…no, I can't even believe that's a possibility.*

"Know better, huh?" I nod. "Sounds like you have her on a pretty short leash." I grin at this description. *It's pretty accurate.* "So...tell me about her. What does she like to do besides your list of chores?"

I could punch this sarcastic fuck. But I lean back in the chair, ignoring his attempts to get a rise out of me again. "Let's see...she's taking cooking classes, but only on Tuesdays and Thursdays. She runs, most days at the gym, but she's starting to follow the same path around the Lake I take every morning." Picturing Lucy in her running outfit, I feel my stomach hurt, like *I've* been punched.

"So she's pretty active...in good shape?" I nod. "That's good. I haven't heard of anyone matching her description at the hospitals yet, but if it was a robbery that turned violent...maybe she was able to get away..." He doesn't say what I know he's thinking. That it could've been a rape turned violent.

I squeeze my fists painfully under the table.

12 Her

"I didn't know you felt that way…" I try to speak calmly, quietly. But my heart is racing too. *This is so not the conversation I thought we'd be having.*

Jake puts his hands up, dropping them, laced on the back of his head. He still towers over me, but he's a little calmer. His breathing is anyway. "I know. I've had my whole life to practice hiding how I feel, Lucy. I've become pretty good at it."

"I'm sorry… I shouldn't have come here." I start to get up again.

"I told you to sit, girl." I stop, my feet on the floor, just staring at him. He's ordered me around a little before. I always thought he was testing me, to see if I really wanted to be submissive with Max or was only pretending to like it. *But this is different.* There's no hint of grin or smile in his voice or eyes. I sit back again.

"I should've told you…that first time I saw you. That first Friday. I should've been honest." He keeps his hands on his head, but he shakes it, shrugging. "I should've told you that I was as mad as Max was. That I was as crazy with being jealous and possessive as he was. That *I* would've punished you too for letting that guy touch you." He looks at me, waiting for my reaction.

I don't know what to say. *I'm in a mess. Such a big mess.* And I can't think. I'm too busy trying to ignore how he's making me feel. *I'm responding to him…the same way I do Max. This is all wrong!*

I jump up and push him out of my way. Or try to anyway. He's able to grab my arm easily and push me back down. "I just want to go!"

"No." He doesn't yell it. Doesn't even raise his voice or lower it. It's a simple statement that I have no choice but to stay. I look at him and can't read his face again. "Maybe I shouldn't have told you all this, Lucy. But…" He lets out an angry deep sigh. "But I know that I won't have another chance. And I meant what I said. You should stop questioning everything."

I wait for him to continue, but he only stares at me. "How can I stop?" I put my hands on my stomach without thinking and his hands follow my movement.

"You just decide. One way or another. You know that Max won't change." I nod slightly. I'd convinced myself on the walk over here that I could talk to Max later. *That I could get him to see that there needed to be some changes, especially if…if we're going to have a baby.* But I know I was only fooling myself. Jake nods to my stomach. "If you're carrying his child now, do you really think there's any chance that he would?"

I shake my head and lower my face into my hands, crying again. *I know that there's no chance that things could be any different with Max. It's his way or no way. And if I'm pregnant...Oh God. I don't know how I let this happen...I kept hoping...* My sobs are loud and uncontrolled, shaking me and the sofa, my face on my knees.

13 Him

Jeff opens the door and my dad drops his coat and jacket on the bench. Jeff follows as Dad strides quickly down my hall to where I sit at the table still. "Have you heard anything?" I shake my head and introduce him to Killaney. They shake hands and I nod to Jeff to get a glass for Dad.

He sits as Jeff pours him a drink. He doesn't take it though. Dad's all business. "So what do we know so far?" I fill him in on what Killaney has told me, what my investigator has learned. *So far, not much.*

He shakes his head, taking a first sip. "A robbery makes sense, but then where is she?" I shake my head. He reaches for his phone, glancing at messages. "I'm waiting to hear from a contact I have in the Mayor's office...see if I can get MPU assigned to this quickly." He sounds as frustrated as I am.

He looks around, "Where's Jake?"

I can feel my face clouding, but I try to relax. Killaney is still watching me. He's not even tipsy after all the scotch. "I sent him home. No use having him wait here." I give Dad a look that he seems to understand. He doesn't ask more questions anyway.

But Killaney picked up on the tension. "Who's Jake?"

"My brother. I'd asked him to wait here in case Lucy showed up while Jeff I were out looking for her earlier." I try to sound casual. I try not to let the anger I feel towards Jake enter my voice. Dad looks a little questioning at me too, but I ignore this for now.

Jeff doesn't say anything, even when Killaney looks up at him. *He's a loyal employee and friend.* He knows I don't want to air my family's business. Killaney just grunts at this and writes something down quickly on his notepad.

14 Her

I wasn't aware of Jake sitting next to me. Or of him pulling my upper body onto his lap, my tears staining his jeans. His hands rub from my head down my back, over and over. I wasn't aware of his soothing sounds and touch until my sobs quieted.

I take a last shaky breath and pull my body up, keeping my face covered with my hands. I wipe my cheeks with my palms, but avoid looking at him. He lifts my chin to look though and wipes my wet cheeks with gentle fingers. "You are beautiful when you cry." *Same words Max would use.*

This somehow adds a spark to my sadness. I realize that I'm not only afraid, but angry. Angrier than I've been in a long time. *How dare he?!* I yank my face away and push myself to sitting a little further away on the sofa. "You don't have the right to touch me like that, Jake. Or to say any of that…" My anger is short lived. I end weakly.

He grins at me though. *That's his response? To grin?!* I actually feel my hand moving before I can even think. But he stops my wrist inches from his face. *I was going to slap him?* I swallow. He doesn't let go of my wrist, only squeezes a little harder. "Say you're sorry."

"I...I'm sorry." He squeezes a little more, then drops my hand onto my lap. I look and see that my wrist is a little pink from his fingers, but not like when Max grabs me.

When I look back at him, he has the same grin. But this time, I'm only confused. I don't know what to think or feel. "I shouldn't have touched you. I shouldn't be telling you any of this. You're right." But he turns a little to face me more. "You've made a big mess for yourself, little girl." I catch my breath at being called this by him, but he keeps talking. "You can't keep going on like you're perfectly fine with everything, but then still question it. That's not fair. To Max."

I can feel my anger again. "To Max? What about me?"

His look darkens only a little, the grin stays, but stretches slightly. I can feel my instant reaction. I calm my face, hide my anger. "Yes. To Max. He's never been anything but honest with you, right?" I nod. I know this is true. *I've never questioned what he wanted...only if I could meet his demands.*

"So it's you that's been dishonest with him." I start to open my mouth to protest, but his glare stops me. "You've been hiding from him all these months...your fears, your...your apprehensions about your future, about a baby." His look turns to a cold stare of anger. I shudder a little watching his handsome features turn to stone. "All the while, you've been *trying* to have a baby with him. Now. When you think you *might* actually be pregnant…you choose *now* to come here and talk to me…like this?!"

I breathe my answer, frozen in his stare, "I had to."

Jake leans forward and before I can stop him, he pulls the back of my head, my face to his and kisses me. On the lips. Just a slight pressure. Almost chaste. Just the slightest touching of wet lips together. He slowly moves my head back. I open my eyes. I didn't even realize I'd closed them. Or that I'd held my breath.

"I'll help you, Lucy. Tonight at least. I'll talk to Max."

I lower my head and he gets up to grab his phone. He comes back to sit in front of me with it, but he doesn't make the call yet.

He lifts my chin, gently this time. He grins at me again, but this time it's more like his gentle smile. I don't know how, but I return it. *Jake has this ability to pull me out of myself no matter what is happening.* Even when I was hurting after Max beat me, I was able to laugh with him. I don't remember about what. But I remember that it felt good to laugh, even when it hurt to move.

"But you know I'm not going to be able to convince him to change. Max isn't ever going to change, Lucy…" I only nod. I do know that. Jake sits up a little more. "And you need to decide for yourself if this is really what you want. No more indecision. Because if you *are* carrying his child, I won't be able to help you again." I only blink at him for a moment.

"And if I'm not?"

He just rubs his chin again.

15 Him

My phone vibrates on the table. All eyes fix on it. Jake's white teeth smile up at us. It's a dumb photo he took of himself last year with my phone as a joke.

I don't want to talk to him now, but I don't like how Killaney is looking at me, waiting for me to pick up. I grab my phone and get up, heading outside. When I'm on the terrace and out of hearing, "Yeah. What's up?"

"Lucy's here."

It takes me a moment to comprehend what he just said. *I still don't get it.* "What?"

"Lucy. She's safe. She's here. With me." I feel too much at once to think. I don't even respond. I sit down, slowly. Relief and anger flood my nerves. Jake doesn't say anything more.

I try to breathe. Deep breath in. Out. I swallow. "Where are you?"

"My place." His tone is blank. *Trying for calm.*

"Your place?" I squeeze the phone; I'm surprised that it doesn't break. I stand up again, pacing in front of the low wall, not seeing the skyline. "Tell her to get her *ass* home now." I try for a calm voice, but I'm beyond that. I'm yelling into the phone. I turn and see Dad, Jeff, and Killaney looking in my direction. I turn around again so my back is to them. "Put her on."

"I won't do that, Max." *Red. Pure red.* That's all I see for a moment. "I'm bringing Lucy home. But you need to calm down."

I swallow. "Don't tell me to be calm, Jake. What the fuck!"

"I'll explain it when I'm there. Just…just try to get control of your anger. All right?" He hangs up before I can say anything more.

I turn with my phone raised to throw towards the wall. Dad is standing in the doorway, staring at me. I stop. "What did Jake have to say?"

"Lucy." My teeth are grinding with the words. I can't stop my anger from tearing my lips back, my whole body tensed to hit something. "She's with him. At his place. He's bringing her here now."

16 *Her*

I can hear Max's voice. I can hear him yelling into Jake's phone. I put my hands over my ears. Too scared to move, even when Jake puts the phone down on the coffee table next to him.

Jake pulls my hands away from my head and I finally look at him. His face is neutral. A mask I've seen before, when he's around a lot of people or family, when he doesn't want to show how he feels, or he's getting control of his anger. I think he's trying to be calm for my sake. I almost laugh, a little jerk of a gruff sound escapes my lips. I frown at him.

"We need to go. Now." I only nod. His voice is commanding. A deep, dark voice…I'm familiar with its sound…an echo I've heard many times from my husband.

"I…I need to use your bathroom first…" He nods down a dark hall. I stumble up, feeling a crazy amount of lead in my legs. I'm dizzy with fear. *I don't know if I can face Max right now. And all that's happened here with Jake...I've made such a mess*. I just keep thinking this same thing over and over.

I get to the bathroom and turn on the light. After peeing, I just stand in front of the counter, staring at myself for a second. I splash a little cold water on my face finally. I'm too scared, too shocked even to cry more. But my body shakes. I grip the counter to stop myself. I laugh. A scary hysterical sound. *Is this what a death row convict feels like? I'm walking to my judgment...*

I head back down the hall. Jake is in the kitchen, just setting down the bottle of beer he finished. He looks strange. A mix of anger and... *And I don't know. Determination? Guilt? I have no idea. I thought I knew him...*

He doesn't look at me, just goes into the bathroom and doesn't bother closing the door. I can hear him pee in the dark. I can hear him wash his hands.

When he comes out, he grabs my arm in a firm grip. The same, tight, almost painful grip from before. "Let's go."

And he keeps this hold all the way down the stairs, out the door, down the block, into a cab. I only stare at him. Trying to see his look budge from the same stern, strong look. It doesn't.

In the cab, he takes my hand and holds it, pulling our hands onto his knee. He doesn't look at me though. He just looks straight ahead.

I've really messed up today.

17 Him

Dad doesn't say anything for a moment. He moves instead to stand in front of me, close to me, blocking any view of me from Jeff and Killaney. "Get ahold of yourself, boy." I have a second of rage at this. He sounds like Jake. But he puts his hand on my arm, the one not holding my phone. His grip has always been like a vise. His voice is calm, in control, commanding as usual. Too many years raised under his belt, his complete power, I don't move.

I want to tell him to fuck off. I thought it plenty of times growing up. *But he's the reason I am who I am. He saved our family. I can't disrespect him no matter what. Even now.*

I take a breath. I lower my phone. I shrug my shoulders and head, loosening up the hold my anger has on my body. I meet his eyes again. I nod.

Dad lets go of my arm. We turn together to head back inside.

Jeff is trying not to show his question. He's trying to look neutral. He saw my anger. So did Killaney.

Killaney raises his eyebrows, waiting. When I'm closer to the table, he finally speaks. "So...news?"

Dad answers for me. He keeps his voice calm, neutral. "Yes. It appears Lucy is with my other son. She's safe and sound."

Killaney doesn't stop appraising me though. I walk by him into the kitchen to give myself a few more moments alone with my anger.

18 Her

Jake takes my elevator card from me. He hasn't let go of my arm again, a firm grip, pushing and pulling me along. *I guess this makes him my executioner.* He's walking me to face Max's anger.

I'm numb. I'm not really sure that I'd be able to walk without his holding me up, without his strong force moving me along. I keep staring at him, trying to see any change in his expression. So far, he's been this strange mix of anger and determination. But somehow neutral too, his looking through me look, with only a touch of anger. But I don't know if it's directed at me or Max...*probably both.*

Just before the elevator door opens on the top floor though, he turns his head slightly to me. And he grins again. I'm weak. I lean against the wall, pulling on his arm, but the doors open at the same time and he yanks me forward.

I can see that our door is ajar. Jake pauses for a second, pulling me closer to him. He whispers to me, an angry edge, a command not to be argued with, "Shut up. Not a word until I tell you to speak." I only nod, but he doesn't even wait for this. He leads me into the apartment.

As we walk down the hall, I'm aware of two things. *Silence. And a face I don't know*. The other three faces are all angry. Ron, Jeff...*and Max*. I swallow, looking down quickly to avoid eye contact with anyone.

Jake doesn't let go of my arm, keeps it close to his chest, hiding his grip though.

19 Him

I imagined all sorts of ways tonight would end. I didn't allow myself to imagine the worst cases. The ones where Lucy didn't walk in that door... but this? Fuck! I never thought I'd see my brother holding the arm of my wife... Where's she been? And what the hell has she been up to since this afternoon?

Jake nods at Dad, but doesn't say anything. He stays close to Lucy. *She at least has the decency to look ashamed, to look down.* I step forward, but Dad speaks first. His words halt me.

"Lucy. It's good to see you're safe and sound. You had us all worried, girl." Dad moves to put his hands on her shoulders and kiss her cheek. She looks scared, pressing more into Jake's side.

Jake answers, nudging her. "She was stuck in my elevator this whole time. I really need to get that damn thing fixed." Her half smile at the nudge quickly disappears and she looks down again.

Dad doesn't respond, just moves so I can see his look of warning, his back to Killaney and Jeff. I nod before he's turned enough to not block their view of me anymore.

I move forward, ignoring Jake and Lucy. "Looks like you were right, Killaney. The wife always does show up in these cases…" I try for a light-hearted laugh, but I know I fall far short of this. I nod to Jeff, who stands.

Killaney stays seated though, looking from me to Lucy behind me. "Mrs. Traeger? Do you mind answering a few questions?"

I don't turn to see Lucy's face, and I don't wait for her to respond. "Thought you weren't *technically* on duty, Detective?"

He flicks his eyes to me again. "You're right." He smiles. "I can come back tomorrow if you'd prefer something more formal, Max."

I shake my head and lift my hands open in front of me. I sit down at the table to face Killaney. He has a clear view of Lucy now; my back is still to her. I don't trust keeping my anger in check if I look at her. I can picture her look of fear and how her body tried to shrivel seeing me.

I watch Jeff's face. He stays standing, but doesn't move away from the table.

20 Her

I shake in Jake's hold. Thankfully, Max moves away. I can't see his face. I can see that his body is tense, filled with anger still. But for some reason he's pretending to be calm. So is Ron. He's still standing close to us and looking so stoic.

This only makes me shake more. I can feel Jake's hand gripping harder. I steal a glance up at him, but he doesn't look away from the short man at the table.

Jake leads me to sit and he takes a seat right next to me. I'm glad that he stays close. Max is to our right, the other man is to our left.

"Mrs. Traeger, I'm Detective Killaney…a friend of Jeff's." The man nods up towards Jeff, who's standing a little ways down the table. "Your husband and Jeff called me to check up on you after they found your purse… They thought something might've happened to you…?"

I look at Jake. I know I shouldn't. I can tell by his look, staring straight at this detective, not turning to me, he only nods a little. I quickly look back. "I...I'm sorry that I had everyone so worried."

Jake thankfully speaks up, "Her purse and phone were stolen. Lucy didn't have any money to get home. So she walked to my place. To find me." I can see that he glances at Max. I don't follow his eyes. I can't. "She was stuck in my elevator for hours before I got there."

I don't say anything. *That was a partial lie, a partial truth. I'm not a good liar. I won't be able to lie to Max if he questions me. I don't know what I was thinking...stupid!*

"That must've been some ordeal, Mrs. Traeger?" Killaney leans forward. I only nod. I notice that his breath has alcohol. I take in the empty glasses and nearly empty bottle on the table too.

For some reason, this makes me angry. *While he was so worried about me, Max sat around here drinking?*

I stand up, grabbing the glasses quickly as I do; they clink together loudly. I head into the kitchen, walking by Ron as I do. I ignore his stern look.

I make noise putting the glasses in the sink angrily. I return, but don't sit down again. I stand away from everyone, with my arms crossed. "If you don't mind...it's been a long day..."

I don't know where this is coming from. How I'm able to stand, let alone come across as upset with everyone. *It's like I'm watching myself from afar. I can see that I want to get this over with. I want to get to the part where...No. I'm not brave enough to say that...the part where Max can unleash the anger he's holding in....There. I said it.* I shake again though, all bravery gone.

Max gets up. I look at Jake, but see that he's wearing his neutral mask, only the hint of a shake to his head is given to me.

Max comes to stand right next to me, putting his arm gently around me. He kisses my head and I melt into his arm for a moment. *His gentleness...it's what I crave most right now.* "Lucy's right. I'm going to have to ask everyone to leave. I appreciate your staying...and helping. But she's home where she belongs now." He looks at me and I can see the dark look he's burying. "And she needs to get to bed."

Jeff moves to leave, nodding at Killaney. Killaney reluctantly gets up, putting his notepad away.

He stops in front of us though. "I'll have prints on her phone tomorrow or the next day at the latest. I'll let you know if we find anything. But you'll need to come file a report with the precinct too." I see Max nod. Killaney keeps staring at me, but I keep my look composed. I don't know how. But I manage not to shake or cry or scream. *Only in my head.*

21 Him

I move my arm from around Lucy to grab her arm and turn her to me, not rough, not gentle. She drops her arms to her sides, but doesn't look up into my eyes. "Look at me, little girl." She does. Her usual responsiveness.

But Jake stands and moves to be next to us. I can see Dad coming back from closing the front door to join us too.

It's like watching a bad movie. You can see everything happening, but you can't make it better.

I let go of Lucy's arm. "Where were you this afternoon?"

She doesn't stop staring, but it's Jake that answers. "I told you. Her purse was stolen and she was stuck in my old elevator."

I move just my eyes from him to her. A few times. Dad is now on the other side of Lucy. *A tight little circle.* I laugh. "Not buying it." I look at Lucy again. "Tell me where you were, Lucy. Now!" She jumps at the rise in my voice. *Good.*

But Jake is still interfering. "I told you…"

Dad shuts him down this time. "Jake. Stay out of this." Lucy is the only one who doesn't look at Dad. I can see Jake wants to argue, but he doesn't say anything more.

"Answer me, little girl." I say this quietly, in a deep, demanding voice. *One I know she'll respond to quickly.*

22 Her

It's my downfall. Not being able to lie to him. I thought I could. Max would see right through me. And this is my one chance to get him to see...

I swallow, not taking my eyes off him. "I needed to talk to Jake." I watch as his face slowly melds...into the angriest face I saw one time before. Somehow made more horrible by the calmness, the lack of change in his body. It's all on his eyes and lips. And I want to run again. My heart leaping into my throat, I have to hold back a cry. I put my hand to my mouth though.

But this time, we're not alone. Jake sees this change too. I can feel him press a little closer. And Ron turns to face Max a little more.

How strange. I can hear every breath, feel every tension. How long have we stood like this? I start to see pops of bright lights in front of a darkening curtain. I stagger a little and feel hands on my arms. I look down and can't tell if they belong to Jake or Max. *Oh, I see... both.*

I'm pulled towards a chair and sat down hard. I want to say, "Thank you," but my mouth's not working... *all fuzzy right now.* I cover my face and try to follow the words said behind me. But I really just need to breathe for a moment.

23 Him

Shit. She's going to faint. I don't drop my anger, but I grab her arm to stop her legs from buckling under. Jake grabs her other arm. I look from his hand on my wife to his face. He's not letting go. We pull her over to the table and put her in a chair.

"What the fuck is going on, Jake?" I can see Dad moving to stand near us again. I ignore him.

"She was scared of you." Jake matches my tone, says this like it's an accusation. An explanation. *It's not.*

"So? She runs to you?"

Jake lowers his eyes to Lucy's head. I don't need to look down to see that she's trying to get her breathing under control again, covering her face and shaking. He tries for a calmer, more even tone, "She didn't run to me, Max. She needed a friend to talk to. That's all. I didn't make it home…she got stuck in my elevator. That's it." He tries to shrug like this is no big deal.

My tone hasn't changed. I'm only getting angrier. "Let me get this straight…she left here for her appointment, but instead went to *your* place…looking for *you*?" He only nods, keeping his eyes on me again. For a moment I can't see beyond the red. *I can't believe any of this is happening.*

My nightmare earlier tonight was someone holding Lucy for a ransom or taking her and…and hurting her. But this? That she was with my own brother?

Dad interrupts, "Jake, why would Lucy go to your place?" He's angry too, but trying to sound calm like Jake.

Jake doesn't look at him as he answers, just keeps staring at me, "I've been talking with Lucy…for a few months now. We've become *close* friends." I don't like the way he stressed the word. My jaw and fists clench harder. "She was scared about her doctor's appointment today and she needed a friend to talk to." He repeats what he's already said. *It's not an explanation!*

Jake finally takes his eyes off me and looks at Dad. "She's been scared for a while. She just needed a friend…" Dad shakes his head slightly, but I can see that he's out of words too. Jake fills in the silence again. "It was stupid. She knows this. She knows she shouldn't have…" He glances at me, but lowers his eyes to Lucy again quickly. "She would've been home sooner, if it weren't for my elevator. I found her when I left here and brought her back as soon as I could."

Dad sighs. It's a sound we've heard before, with a look we've seen. It's a resolute sound and look. He doesn't like what he's heard, but he's done listening. *So am I.* I don't wait for him to speak.

"Thanks for bringing my wife home where she belongs, Jake." Sarcasm and anger mix to clip each word. He shoots me a look filled with volumes, but doesn't say anything back. "Lucy." She doesn't move. I look down at her and repeat her name a little louder to get her to look up. "Go to our room."

She pushes herself to stand, but Jake grabs her arm again, pulling her closer to him. "No."

I narrow my eyes, anger taking a backseat to disbelief for a second. Only a second. "Get your hand off my wife, Jake." I don't move. I don't need to, we're all standing very close.

Jake drops his hand, but Lucy stays standing against his arm. My brother stares at me; I stare back. I'm pretty sure he wants to hit me. *I know I want to hit him.*

Dad breaks in, "Lucy. Go sit on the sofa." No one argues with his commands. Lucy meekly moves two steps back and turns to the living room. I don't take my eyes off Jake, but I see her sit on the edge, watching us. "Jake. Max. Sit." We don't move. "Now!" *That did it.* We both sit at the table, slowly, still staring at each other.

24 Her

This is so much worse than I could've imagined. All three Traeger men, here, angry. All because of me. I want to cry and cover my face. But it's a train wreck I can't look away from. I can only stare.

Ron takes the seat I was just in, between Max and Jake. "This has been a long day for everyone. I have a few phone calls to make to clear up this mess." His voice booms like Max's. His anger a film covering everyone. "Max. You need to see to your wife. She's obviously had some sort of shock or something today." He speaks slowly, "She needs to be dealt with...*gently* tonight." Max looks at him, but takes a while before he nods.

"Jake." I watch as Max looks at his brother again; Jake turns to look at Ron. "You need to go home. And think about how your involvement here tonight only made matters worse...for everyone."

"I'm not leaving until I hear Max say that he won't hurt her." I shiver hearing this. Jake is calm, but his voice has the same edge, the same steely grit as Ron's. I want to jump up and run. I want to cower behind Jake. I want to beg Max to forgive me. *I just want to hide really.*

Max laughs. It's a choked sound, sandpaper against bricks sound, "*You're* trying to tell me what I can and can't do, little brother?" *Oh, God. This is only getting worse.*

Ron puts his hand on both men's arms on the table. "Enough." I can see how he has an effect on them. Grown men, but they're both still under his control. I can see myself in them, under Max's control. *Always.* "Max, that detective is going to want to check on Lucy, to get a report tomorrow. It'd be best if you kept your anger in check right now, son." Max again only nods.

Ron turns to Jake. "I told you to go home. Now." Jake finally nods too and gets up slowly.

He walks over to me, standing close, hiding me from Max and Ron for a moment. He puts his finger on my cheek, tracing a tear I didn't know was there. "I'll call you tomorrow. You'll be fine." I only swallow in response, still too afraid to speak. My arms are wrapped around me, trying to hold my fear in, keeping myself safe. It's futile. But his words do make me feel better; it's a lie I hold onto it.

Jake walks down the hall and I can hear the door quietly open and close. I can't help but look back at the table. Ron and Max are both staring at me with the same look. Disgusted anger. Shocked anger. Furious anger.

I'm too frightened to move or breathe or blink. I just keep holding onto Jake's words...*I'll be fine.*

25 Him

I close the front door.

Dad stayed long enough to send Lucy to bed and make the calls he needed. I had to sit and listen as he explained that it was just an accident. That Lucy is fine and back home. No, no need to investigate anything. She was only trapped in an elevator for hours, but she's fine now.

I had to listen to Dad laugh and charm his way out of the favors he pulled for me. The number of people he had already involved, he didn't waste any time. If Lucy hadn't shown up when she did, my house was minutes from being a full-blown TV-style crime scene investigation.

I sigh. *I know he's right. I have to keep my anger in check. For tonight anyway.* There may still be questions to answer tomorrow. Too many people involved.

For Dad's sake. For my sake. I can't let my anger have control. If I punish Lucy tonight... I have to stop myself from thinking this. The images that pop into my head are too vivid. *My hands ache to punish her!*

I take a deep breath and walk down the hallway. I stop at our bedroom door. *I can't go in there. If I see her now...I won't be able to stop myself.*

I turn and walk into the guest room instead and close the door quietly.

26 Her

I don't remember falling asleep. I'm still in my clothes, on top of the covers. *It's late. 3:00 a.m.* I don't need to roll over to know Max isn't in bed with me. But the house is quiet. I don't know where he is.

I get up and head to the bathroom. The lights hurt for a second, making me blink my puffy, red eyes. I splash more water on my face, take off my clothes, put on my robe and nothing else.

I don't have a plan. I'm not really thinking. Just going on instinct. *Maybe…*

I quietly open the door. I can see the guest room door is closed. *Max must be in there.*

I take a deep breath. Steeling myself. *I can do this. I have no choice…I have to face him sooner or later…*

I quietly open the door and hear his deep breathing. I hesitate. I second guess. *Maybe I should just let him sleep…not wake the monster…I'm trying to joke to myself?…so not funny!*

I stand over the bed, putting my hand on his dark, soft waves. I gently rub his head, "Max…come to bed, sweetie…"

He's awake in an instant, rolling over and grabbing me with him. He's on top of me before I can even squeal at the sudden movement. "You want me to come to bed, baby?" I only nod. I don't know if he can see me even.

I can't see his face, his shoulders block the light from the hallway. But I can hear the edge in his voice still. *I'd hoped waking him quietly, gently…a foolish hope that he'd respond gently too.*

I feel his hand inside my robe, pushing it open. I can feel him hard against my leg already. I can't help myself. My body is a traitor. I respond and arch to meet his hand between my legs. He roughly shoves two fingers in, his knuckles punching against me. I cry out, but he only repeats the slamming in and out several times. I know better than to try closing my legs. I've made that mistake before. I don't resist. I just cry out with each thrust. He finally pulls his fingers out and I shudder with pain…and that traitorous wet excitement I always feel with his touch, good or bad.

"On your belly." I try to obey, but my robe is trapped under us. He lifts off a little and I get my arms out. I slowly roll over. He grabs my hair and yanks my head back. "Spread your legs, whore." *He hasn't called me that…not since that night.* I know he thinks I betrayed him again today. I open my legs. He laughs. "You can do better than that." I open further and he lets go of my hair.

"I'll give you a choice, little girl." I shiver hearing his words. I thought he'd move to be between my legs, not leave me exposed like this. "I promised not to beat you...*tonight* anyway. But that doesn't mean that I won't hurt you." I muffle a little cry into the bed. "But I'll give you a choice now. I plan to beat you with the buckle of the belt...up and down." His fingers trace goose bumps from my legs to my shoulders. I shake and cry into the bed more. "But I'll relent...only beat you with the leather...if you tell me now that you deserve to be fucked hard in your ass. Like a good little whore needs."

Oh God. He did this on our honeymoon. I remember the pain. But...but he's never hit me with the buckle before...I can't take that...I can't. "Please..."

"Please, what, little girl?"

I can't say it. He's made me beg for punishment before. He's made me tell him exactly what I did wrong to deserve his anger. *But this...* "Please..."

"I'm losing patience, Lucy...you've just earned the buckle on your ass no matter what you say...wanna save your pretty back and legs that pain? Then tell me what you deserve, whore."

"Please...do...do my bottom..." *I know better than to curse, to say it the way he did. Even in my rabbit holed-brain, I know better than to anger Max more that way.* I push my mind away, trying to not feel his body move to be above me, between my legs.

But I feel everything. There's no escaping. He spreads my cheeks with his thumbs. I can feel the tip of his hard cock against me and I try to squeeze my body smaller, away. He laughs. "Go ahead. Tense up. I'll only like it more." He pushes a little, but not in. "I'm not going to make this easy on you, whore. I'm not going to make you wet. I want this to hurt you." He pushes in fast and hard.

I scream. I'm being ripped apart. A searing pain, I try to push up and get him off. I don't have control over myself, it's instinct to fight against this pain. But he doesn't budge. His legs stay locked next to me, his cock buried deep. He shoves my arms down and holds me against the bed. "I like when you move. Pushes me in deeper."

He pulls out a little and I cry more. He's almost out and I take big gulps of air and hair, my face smashed to the side, my hair covering me. "Tell me you want it. Tell me you *deserve* it."

I know he'll only hurt me more if I disobey, if I try to resist. "I want it....I...I deserve..." my tears cover the last word. My cry strangles it when he shoves into me again.

He leans forward, pushing his cock down and making me cry out louder. With his lips gently against my ear, "Move your hips. Push yourself against me." I'm too shaky to do much, but I move my hips up, crying more. "Good whore. You do like it, don't you?" He kisses my ear and raises up. He thrusts in and out fast several times, then slows down. I can hear his breathing over my cries and grunts. I know he's slowing down to stop himself from coming too fast.

"Please..."

He stops, his cock deep in me. "Squeeze me then. Make me come, whore." I shake my head against the bed. "Do it or I'll come now, get hard and fuck your ass all over again."

"Please, Max…please…" But I close my eyes, squeezing them as much as my ass. I cry out, letting go.

"Again." I don't know how, but I do. My cries are constant, shaking the bed, us. I don't know if I let go; it feels like I just hold onto him, a desperate embrace of sobs and pain.

I feel him explode, his legs rocking the bed and me. But he doesn't get out. He stays in me, rubbing my head and back. When my sobs finally quiet. He leans over, pulling out and kissing me cheek through my hair, "That's my good whore."

He gets up and I roll over, waiting until he leaves the room to really cry. My body convulses with sobs. I don't hear him when he returns. "Get up." I jump at his voice. But my sobs are silenced. I shakily get off the bed, grabbing my robe. It's still clean even if I'm not. I wrap this around me and slowly walk out. I feel my asshole is the size of my ass and I can feel his come dripping out of me. I have to stop myself from throwing up. I take a few deep breaths before I walk into our bedroom.

He's in the bathroom. I can hear the shower running. I walk in slowly. He's already cleaning himself off, his beautiful hair slicked back, his muscled body bubbled with soap. He sees me and opens the door. His eyes are still hard, but he doesn't say anything. I let the robe drop to the floor. I'm numb.

The warm water feels good for a moment, a shock against my numbness. He hands me the soap and turns away while I clean myself. I wince at the pain, trying to be gentle. When I turn around, he's staring at me again.

But his face has changed a little. The anger's still there. But so is pain. He's had this look before. Like he wants to cry but he won't let himself. "Why?"

I don't know how to respond to this. His voice takes on more volume over the water. "Why would you betray me like that, Lucy?"

"I...I'm sorry...I wasn't trying...I didn't mean to hurt you..." My voice echoes and I can hear how pathetic I sound. I'm hurt, but I'm the one apologizing to him. *This is just the way it is with us.*

He moves slowly to stand in front of me. He puts his hands on my shoulders, gently. But I don't trust that he'll stay gentle. I can see the dark anger; I can still hear it. His body is still tense. "Haven't I always told you exactly what I expect of you?"

"Yes" This is true. From the beginning, he's told me how it has to be with us. His demands were never a secret he hid. *Jake's right; I'm the one who's been hiding.*

"Then you know you've been very bad, little girl." It's not a question. I don't move. He said he wouldn't punish me today, but I'm suddenly very cold in the steamed shower.

He turns off the water and opens the door. I follow him out. He puts a towel around me and dries off my hair and back. He kisses my forehead and even smiles at me as he turns to get his own towel. I'm too numb, scared, confused. *I don't know what to make of any of this.*

When he's dry, he takes the towels and hangs them up. I watch as he gently takes my hand and leads me back to the bedroom. I watch as he gets under the covers, propped up on pillows and pats my side of the bed. I slowly get in. My butt still hurts and I wince as I put pressure on it, lying on my side quickly. He puts his arms around me and pulls me onto his chest more.

I'm still not trusting, but this has always been our routine. He punishes me, then comforts me. I'm used to kissing my own tears on his chest, feeling his heartbeat against my cheek. I put my hand up on his stomach and feel his breaths, his muscles. I can see that he's aroused again under the sheet. I can feel my own body respond to his gentle touches. *I'm a damn lab rat in his maze, doing whatever I can for a piece of cheese.*

I decide I have nothing to lose. If he's going to keep his promise of not hurting me more, then it's now or never. "Max?"

"Yes, baby." He sounds almost sleepy.

"I…I don't want to make you angrier with me…but…"

27 Him

"…but I need to talk…to say something…?"

I can feel her shaking against me. *My little Lucy. She knows she's in a lot of trouble.* She's never made me this angry before. Not even that night when she let Rich touch her. She's been on her best behavior ever since. *I don't understand why she blew it. Why she misbehaved so badly.*

"Go on."

She moves her head up to look at me more. I kiss her nose. I've always loved her nose, so straight and little. *I'll keep my promise…I'll never break her, never cause her any real damage.* But I smile thinking of the black eye I'm going to give her tonight. *I won't use my fist. Her nose will be safe.*

She swallows and takes a deep breath. "I am sorry for everything." I nod. *Of course she is. She's sorry she's in so much trouble.* "It was stupid and foolish…and I shouldn't have done any of it…" I nod again, but I'm curious where she's going with this. *Does she really think that apologizing now while I've promised not to punish her will help to ease my anger? She should know better by now.*

"I know you know…" She stops, I can feel her body heat up again, her heartbeats flittering thumps against my side. She continues in a tiny voice, "…about Jake coming here…" I keep myself relaxed, not responding to the mental image and shouting in my own head at her words.

"And I'm sorry for keeping that a secret too." I nod, continuing to stroke her hair and back. "I needed someone to talk to. After…after what you did…that night…"

"What I did?" I keep my voice steady, but I can feel my own body getting warmer now.

"…Yes…when you hurt me so badly…when I couldn't move without pain for a week…" Her voice rises slightly, an unpleasant note of defiance in it.

"Careful, little girl…"

I feel her squirm, swallowing and moving her head back down. When she starts again, her voice is small and soft once more, "I was in a lot of pain…and I was scared, Max."

"Didn't I tell you what would happen if you let another man touch you again?"

"…Yes, but…" She's shaking again, I can feel her tears on my chest, her fingers fidgeting against my stomach. I wait for her to continue, wanting to see how far she's willing to push this. "But…I never thought you'd be able to hurt me like that…that you'd even *want* to hurt me that badly…"

I lift her chin up to look at me again, but I'm gentle. I even keep my voice soft, my look tender. "I'm going to hurt you worse than that later today, little girl."

She's shocked. I like seeing her looks as they change so quickly. Shock. Fear. Guilt. Despair. And one I haven't seen in a long time. Anger.

It doesn't matter. She'll be feeling only fear and guilt soon enough. And pain.

28 Her

"I can't…I can't believe you're saying…" I try to breathe. *I must be in a nightmare…today must've been a nightmare and I'll wake up soon, right? He can't be looking at me so sweetly and saying…this!*

"I think I've been too lenient with you, Lucy. It's my own fault really. I've given you too much time to think. I've not demanded enough of you, to keep you busier." He smiles at me. I feel his hand move from my hip around to gently press against my lower stomach. "That'll change soon if you're pregnant." He shrugs. "And I'll keep a closer eye on you. I won't let you get yourself into so much trouble again, little girl."

I push against him quickly, shoving myself away before he can react. I'm standing, naked. Furious. Shaking with anger at his words.

"Do you hear yourself? Max…I'm practically a prisoner here *now*. I threw my phone away because I know you trace my every move, my every call. I needed a minute to myself. To breathe! To think!"

His look doesn't change much. He remains sweet with a hint of anger, but his words carry even more edge. The warning edge. "You want time to think? How bout thinking about what you've done wrong? Yesterday and now. How bout thinking about how you've disappointed me?"

I take a breath, but stay standing away from him. I try to think. *How can I get him to see that I need him to talk to me seriously?* "I…I know I disappointed you, Max. And I *am* sorry. I already said I'm sorry for everything that's happened." I take another deep breath, trying to see if any of this is getting through to him. *I can't tell.* "But…but I've been struggling for so long with…with everything. I need to talk to you. I need you to *listen* to me…please?!" My tears run down my cheeks freely, I brush them away angrily.

"What is it you think I *need* to hear? What is it you think you *need* to say, Lucy?"

"I…I'm afraid."

"You said that already." He's calm, matter-of-fact almost. "You *should* be afraid."

"Max…" I'm running out of words. My shock, fear, and anger zap any thoughts. I swallow and start over, trying for a stronger voice again.

29 Him

"I'm afraid that you don't really love me…that you only love how you can order me around…and…and hurt me." She swallows again. I let her have this time to speak. *No harm in letting her talk as long as she's calm about it*. "I'm afraid…if we have a child…how you'll want to raise our child…" She stops. Her mouth opening and closing, but she only tries to breathe, her hands against her stomach.

I speak calmly, slowly, in the voice I use when I want to be very clear with her, a child needing a reminder lesson. "Lucy. I love you very much. Everything about you. I've loved you since the beginning." I put my hand out and pat the bed again. She doesn't move at first, but she responds when I lower my brows a little more. She sits on the edge of the bed, but still away from me.

"I do love ordering you around as you put it. And I do love being able to hurt you." I can see she tenses up again, almost standing, but she stops herself. I keep my voice very calm, very slow still. "And I will raise our children to be respectful of me and of you. Our children will know that I'm in charge and they will fear being punished if they misbehave." She starts to shake her head, but I continue. "But understand…that my harshest, strictest lessons…and discipline…I reserve for *you*."

I give her a moment to think about this. "I expect full obedience and submission from you, Lucy. No questions. No arguments. No negotiations. You know this, little girl. You mess up, I *will* punish you. And from now on…I *will* be harder on you."

I can see her eyes fill with tears. *So pretty*. Her hair down her front, her hands in her lap. I reach and pull her towards me, not giving her a chance to stand up again. She doesn't resist. I pull her into my chest, a tight ball with her knees up and pressed against me. I pull the covers over us and hold her.

30 Her

I try to be still in his arms. I'm too chilled by his words. So calm. So clear.

"What if…what if that's not what I want…what I need…?" I say this as almost a whisper, too afraid to say it; too afraid to keep it in.

Max doesn't say anything for a long time, just keeps stroking his hand from the top of my head, down my back, across my raised legs and back again. I almost think he didn't hear me until his voice answers in a whisper too, "You gave up having a choice when you became my wife, Lucy. What you want…what you need…*I* decide. You'll take whatever I do to you."

Even in a whisper, I know his final tone when I hear it. *There's no point in talking more.*

Jake was right. He'll never change. I swallow and still only speak in a cracked whisper, "What…what are you going to do to me, Max?"

And he waits to answer me again. His voice slides across the words, like he's enjoying hearing the fear in my voice, feeling the shiver in my body. "Do you really want to know, little girl?"

"I…I might be pregnant…" It's all I can think to say, hopeful that he'll snap out of this deeper darkness still. *Foolish hope. And coward. Too afraid to hear what he has planned for me.*

"Yes. I think we should get you a new appointment later today." He moves us both down the bed. "Enough talking. Get some sleep now, baby." He kisses the top of my head and relaxes his arms a little.

31 Him

I didn't fall back asleep after last night. I stayed awake, listening to Lucy's breathing eventually even and deepen. Just that was enough to make me almost sleep. I'm always calmer having her next to me.

And I could use some calming right now. It's why I got out of bed at 5:00 a.m. and went for a longer run. It's why I'm still sitting on the terrace with a cold cup of coffee, thinking.

Yesterday seems like a nightmare. Not knowing where Lucy was. Looking for her. Talking to Killaney, Dad, Jeff. Jake... but I skip over him for now. Everything that happened up until she was home again, safe.

I've never felt helpless before. A feeling I hope never to feel again. *That Lucy made me feel this way...I can't forgive her. Not yet anyway. Not until I've punished her.*

Which leads to my next frustration. Having to wait to punish her. *I don't like waiting for anything.* I see the reason, the sense in waiting. But that doesn't mean I like it. It's been a long time since I've had to wait for anything. *Waiting last night to hear from Lucy...I need to stop thinking about it.*

Since Jake called, since knowing what happened to her, I've had to hold my anger in check. I've had to stop my hands from wringing her neck. From punching him. I look at my hands holding the cold cup now.

I don't know that I'll be able to forgive Jake for his part in all this. I'll try, but it'll be a long time before I trust him again with Lucy.

I smile. *But that doesn't matter.* I've already arranged for a new driver for me. Jeff will be keeping Lucy company from now on. She won't be leaving here without me knowing where she is at all times. And no one will be allowed in here without my permission.

She said last night that this was practically her prison. *Well, baby, it is now.* I smile. *For her own sake, I hope she takes these new rules well.* She's already in for a world of hurt for what she's done and said.

What kept me up...what robbed my sleep wasn't any of these thoughts, though.

It was the same thoughts I've had before. About Lucy.

I knew she struggled. When I'd see her resisting or trying to work around a demand, I'd be stricter and more severe with her. It's when I'd be my most cruel. *I don't really want to be cruel to her. I like hurting her, sometimes just for my pleasure…but I want to be loving and kind to her too. And most of the time, I am.*

I give her all of my love. I deny her nothing, within reason anyway. I'm not a fool though. I know what I demand isn't for everyone. I've had enough girlfriends throw modern feminism and equal rights crap in my face to know that Lucy isn't like any other girl.

She understands that she needs my guidance, my devotion to making her the best wife she can be. She gets that all of my rules, demands, punishments are meant to help her, to help us. To be happy.

So why does she still resist? Why is she still struggling? Why did she run to Jake?

Jake. Fuck! I don't want to think about him. Her. Them.

Holding her last night, trying to sleep, then giving up. *I almost thought about not punishing her…well, punishing her only lightly anyway. I thought it might be easier on us both.*

I know that allowing myself to express the amount of anger I felt yesterday…*that it's dangerous. For her and me.* I didn't picture just using a belt on her. Using the buckle. *I've never done that.* Ron never even used it on us. *Maybe on Mom…I'll have to ask him.*

But before I could stop myself, I pictured hitting her too. Really hitting her. Punching her face, breaking open her cheek, her lips. I pictured choking her hard enough to leave my fingerprints on her pretty neck. I pictured breaking her beautiful nose, so she'd always have a reminder of what would happen if she ever did anything like this again. *I pictured letting myself be out of control.*

She lied to me. Threw her phone away to hide from me. Ran off to be with my brother. Talked back. Argued. Disobeyed almost every rule.

No wonder I'm so angry. But...but I'm worried. I don't want to lose control of myself. I can't. It's a promise I've made to myself.

I know I'm a monster. I've come to terms with this. I don't care what anyone thinks of me. I only care about Lucy, about her obeying and submitting to me.

If I let myself the freedom to really punish her...how I know she deserves to be punished for everything she's done...I don't think I can. *I know I can't. I made a promise to her too. I'll always keep my promises to her. To myself.*

But how do I punish her then? How do I hurt her only a little for all of this?

Maybe I just need a little more time...to calm down more...maybe that will help.

I look at my watch. *I better get her awake.* I made an appointment for her online, we need to get going.

I smile. Another reason to wait to punish her. *She may be carrying my child...I wouldn't want anything to risk that.*

32 Her

I hear Max get up. I stay quiet in bed, waiting for the front door to close behind him. I don't know how long I have, but I breathe a little easier being alone.

I roll over. 5:20 a.m. I hesitate for only a second. I may not have another chance today. I move over to Max's side of the bed, to the phone.

It takes too many heartbeats for him to pick up, his voice sluggish with sleep…maybe alcohol. "Hello?"

"Jake? I'm sorry to call so early…" I whisper even though I know Max is gone.

"Lucy? Are you okay?" Jake sounds wide awake now.

"I…I am. For now, anyway." I try not to think about what Max said last night. "I…wanted to tell you that I made a decision. You told me to make up my mind…and I…I think I have."

"Overnight? Just like that?"

Not what I was expecting from him. I thought he'd be supportive, not sarcastic and angry. "Yes. Just like that." I try for strong, but I can hear how petulant I sound even to me. I go back to whispering, "I don't have long to talk…I think Max went for a run, but I don't know how long before he'll be back."

"Did he hurt you last night?" His dark, deep voice is so protective, so angry. And so like Max's I want to cry hearing it.

I don't want to tell him about what Max did. "No…I'm okay…" I swallow loudly. "I know he'll never change. What he was saying last night…I'm scared. I mean…I'm more scared than I've ever been of him, Jake! I need to get somewhere safe…to get away from him."

I hear him breathe out heavily. It seems to take him forever to answer me. "What you're asking of me, Lucy…I…I want to help you. Shit!" He breathes again in and out, his mouth close to his phone. "I *will* help you, girl. But you have to be honest with me. No bullshit." I wait, not sure what he means. "If I step in…if I interfere more than I already have…and you decide to change your mind and stay…it'll be a lot worse for you…and me. You know that, right?"

"Yes." My whisper is a long hiss of air out.

"You really want to leave Max? To walk away from him? From everything you have with him? You really think you can do that?"

"I…I…" I start to cry, choking on words. "I don't know what else I can do!"

"Shhh…no more tears, Lucy…shhh." I try to sniffle in my sobs, try to stop my body from shuddering more on the bed. I pull my knees up, putting my arm around them. I look up at the ceiling. *Oh God. To never be in this room again? To never feel Max's arms around me again? I can't…*

"I don't know, Jake. I love him…but I can't take all of his anger…it's too much. If you'd seen him…heard him last night…" I'm lost in tears again. I drop my head onto my knees and hold the phone like it's Jake's hand. Like it could actually help me right now.

"Lucy!" His sharp, hard near-shout stops my tears instantly. I hiccup from gulping in a sob. "You need to get yourself calm. Now, girl. He's going to be back any minute and he can't find you on the phone with me like this." I know he's right. *That wouldn't be good.* I sniffle a little more. "Good."

He takes a quick deep breath in and I follow his example. "Max is not going to do anything this morning. He made a promise to me and to Dad that he'd calm down. He'd wait to see if you're pregnant." Something in how he said it, like it hurt him to say the words. It hurts me to think them. "So you have a little time. We have a little time to think about what can be done."

"He's going to make me an appointment today with the doctor." I need to know. I know that. But I'm afraid of knowing, of Max knowing really. "What if I *am* pregnant?"

Jake doesn't hesitate. "I'll still help you, Lucy. But Max will never let you leave with his child. You know that. You...you'd be better off trying to figure out how to make...how to make him happy with you again. If you think that's even possible after yesterday..."

I know Jake's right. I've had this same thought. It's why I got up at 3:00 and went looking for Max. To try to appease him. To make up to him. To show him...I don't know. My mind runs from this thought. "Okay...I don't know if I'll be able to call you again..."

"I'll come by later today...to talk to Max again. All right?"

"Okay....Thanks, Jake..." I hang up quietly.

But I do know. *At 3:00 a.m., I wanted to show Max that I'm still his. That I still know that he has every right to be angry with me. That he has every right to punish me however he wants. That he's right...I will take whatever he does.*

God help me. It's what I thought then. Until he scared me with how calmly he said he would hurt me more than he already has. I'm not strong enough to take that...

And what if I am pregnant...it's not just me I have to think about then...

33 Him

Lucy looks scared. Her fingers keep squeezing each other. Her legs keep tapping against the metal drawers, making the paper below her bottom crinkle. She's dressed again, we're just waiting for Dr. Patel to return with results.

I chose her as Lucy's doctor because I knew she'd be discreet and trustworthy. I allowed her to question Lucy privately on her first visit. She understands how our marriage works and she doesn't question it. Her family ran into some trouble when she was still in med school; Dad helped them out. She understands what owing a favor means. She's well aware that I punish Lucy sometimes. She's seen my marks on her. She saw Lucy today, saw how she winced during the exam. She only looked at me, but said nothing.

"Lucy…" In this small room, even trying to keep my voice soft, it booms against the hard surfaces. She looks at me. *My sweet, lovely Lucy.* "It's going to be okay." I smile, trying to relax her. I stand up and take her hand in mine, pulling her against me. "I love you very much. I heard what you had to say earlier too. I know you're scared, baby." I kiss her palms. She usually smiles at this.

"You do?" She's near tears. She has been since we left the apartment.

"Yes. I know…" I breathe in a little, squeezing her hands, rubbing her fingers a little more. "I know you need reassurances." I wink at her. This usually does the trick. She knows that I'm happy with her when I do this. She does relax, but only a little. *Despite everything that's happened yesterday, this morning…I want her to be happy.*

"I'm not going to hurt you. No matter what the results are today." I hear myself saying it. I hadn't decided this. Until now. I listen to myself making this big decision and I know it's right…*for her, for me.* "I won't punish you for yesterday." And I know I won't. Some part of me has decided to keep the monster locked up, away from Lucy, for good. To keep her safe always. *I've made this decision before. I can do this now. Go on, you can admit it to yourself, coward…you're doing it to keep us safe. She ran to Jake for a reason. And you can't lose her.*

Lucy throws herself into my arms, crying out and hysterically shedding tears. I have to brace myself to not let her fall off the exam table.

"It's okay, baby. It's all going to be okay." I lift her wet chin and kiss her wet lips. "You've given me everything, Lucy…everything I've ever asked of you. I can give you this…a little space…a little time." I kiss her again. "We'll have a clean start. Would you like that, little girl?"

She nods, more tears flowing, but her sobs gone now. "Max, I know you love me…I didn't mean it when I said…"

"Shhh…I know…you were scared." I kiss her again, holding her for a second longer against me before looking into her beautiful red-rimmed eyes. "I won't make promises to you…promises I know I might not be able to keep…but I'll try." She nods. "I'll try to be gentler with you. I'll try to give you some…" *This is harder to say. I don't even know if I want to say it, but I know I have to…for her. I can't lose her. My life is lost without her in it. She scared me yesterday, leaving like that. I won't lose her.* "I'll try to give you some control over your day to day, baby…to allow you more…freedom."

"You will?" I nod. She looks scared again. I don't know why. *Because she doesn't believe me? No…*

I smile, grabbing her chin harder. "That doesn't mean I'm going to let you get away with anything, little girl. And you'll have Jeff as your driver from now on, to take you anywhere, to keep you safe." I may give her a little more freedom, but I'll keep tighter tabs on her. She smiles against the pressure of my fingers. *I know my little Lucy so well. We'll be okay.* She nods and sniffs.

Dr. Patel walks in again at that moment. She gives me a look, but doesn't say anything about my hand on Lucy's chin. "Well…I'm used to seeing tears, but usually not until I give the good news." She laughs.

Lucy is wiping her face, still pressed against me though. I keep my arm around her.

"And good news it is. Lucy, Max…Congratulations. You're pregnant!"

I feel Lucy shake and laugh and cry against me. I turn to hold her, bury her face against me. *I'm glad I made my decision. Whatever happens...we're forever linked. Lucy and me.*

And I will keep us safe. And together.

34 Her

On the ride home, hands linked on my knee like always. I keep looking at him. I'm never sick of staring at his handsome features. Chiseled. That's the word used in the trashy novels I read in college.

No matter how hurt. No matter how scared. No matter how confused. I've always responded to him. To his strong looks. His strong voice. *His strong love.*

I've been living in a crazy state. Up. Down. Side to side. Crazy. I let myself release a stream of curses in my head, a dizzying freedom after everything that's happened. *Shit. Damn. Fuck. Shit. Okay....I'm not that creative!* I laugh again and Max takes my hand and kisses it.

I feel like I've been told the guillotine isn't sharp enough and I won't be executed...long live love!

I'm suddenly sick again. Max shouts to his new driver to stop. We pull in sharply to an open space by the curb and I quickly open the door, leaning out and taking in big gulps of air. I don't vomit. *Barely*. I shake with small cries or laughter or both. I shake.

But I feel Max's hand on my back. His gentle, sweet hand.

No matter what else happens. I will always remember this moment.

His child inside me. His loving touch at my discomfort. His attentive command to stop the car just when I need it stopped. That he loves me. I know this. *Right here. Right now. I don't doubt. I won't ever doubt again that Max's love can conquer anything, even my fears and his anger.*

I don't feel the rest. I hear. But I don't feel.

35 Her

I don't need to open my eyes to know that I'm in a hospital room. The smell. The sounds. Beeps, hisses, muffled voices and footsteps, metal on metal clangs in a distance.

I want to drift back to sleep. I don't want to open my eyes. I don't want to see. Or feel.

A single tear escapes my right eye, but I don't feel it until it drops onto my shoulder.

I drift. Thankfully, I drift.

I feel a prick on my arm and I moan. "I'm sorry, honey."

A nurse smiling at me, that's the first thing I see. Her hand presses on the inside of my left elbow. My left arm is lying on a white sheet. Tubes are coming out of my left hand. I follow them up to a bag of clear liquid, and back down. I turn my head a little. My right arm is wrapped. I swallow several times and she brings me a cup with a straw. Cool water hits my throat and I don't think I've loved the feel of anything more in my life.

I cough a little and she plumps up pillows behind me. My face feels funny, like I don't have control of it.

"Your family is going to be very happy to see your baby blues open, honey." She walks towards the door. "I'll get the doctor too." I want to tell her to stop. *Wait. Please!*

But she's gone.

I close my eyes, but the solace of sleep is lost to me. I hold my breath waiting. I keep my eyes closed.

I can hear the door open. It's quiet but the sound from the hall gets louder for a moment.

"It's good to see you awake. How are you feeling?"

It's a stranger, a doctor. I open my eyes. He's youngish, smiling, looking at a chart. He looks nice, clean cut. I vomit on him.

He steps back quickly and goes into the hall, "Nurse!"

But he returns to my side and pulls the sheets to cover the small vomit on the side of the bed. He wipes my face and the front of my gown. I'm too weak to turn away from him. Too numb. He removes his jacket, leaving it on the floor without a care.

A nurse quickly comes in and he directs him to get a maintenance person in here right away.

Then he smiles at me again. *Nice.* I want to cry and apologize, but I'm silent, watching the movie around me. "Feel a little better?"

I only nod. "Do you know where you are?" He puts a light on my eyes and directs me to follow it.

"In the hospital?" My voice cracks. He picks up the cup and straw and holds it for me. "Take small sips." I do, keeping my eyes on him.

"Yes. You were brought in this morning. Do you know your name?"

"Lucy Traeger."

"Good. How about what day it is?"

"Saturday."

"Good, Lucy. You don't have a concussion. You have lacerations…cuts…to your right side. And your wrist and rib are bruised. But you're fine." He pats the bed. "And your baby is fine."

I'm trying to understand what he's saying.

"What happened? Why am…" I cough again, bringing a splitting pain to my head and neck. My right side explodes with hot, throbbing pain. He gives me the straw again. I close my eyes and wait for this to subside a little.

"What's the last thing you remember?"

"Max." Saying his name is a new kind of pain.

"That's…your husband?" *Why is he looking as white as the sheets on this bed now?* I nod, but this only sends shooting pains to my right eye and temple. I lift my fingers to this side and feel gauze and bandages. *No wonder I feel like I'm hearing through a thick cotton blanket.*

"You were in an accident. A car accident. You're fine." He doesn't look as young or as sweet. He looks tired and dragged through something smelly now.

"Where's my husband…Max?!" I don't know why my voice sounds so strange, so high, so panicked. *Well, it's always high, but still…why is this doctor looking at me…like I'm deranged? This isn't a movie, doc…just tell me where he is!*

"You were both in the accident and…and your husband didn't make it…I'm so sorry…"

I blink. Blink. Blink. Blinkblink.

"What…what…" I blink the hot tears down my cheeks. "What….Max! Max!" I yell, despite the pain in my head, my body. I scream his name. *I know Max will come running into this room any second. I know he'll hit this man for lying to me. I know he'll make everything okay. He has to…he has to…Max!*

I watch as the doctor holds my arms down, he yells something at someone. Something is needled into the bag attached to all the tubes attached to me. I keep yelling. *Max will hear me. He'll come for me…I know he…*

36 Her

I don't open my eyes. I don't ever want to open my eyes again. I feel warm, strong fingers around my left hand. I move one finger a little and I hear Jake's voice.

So like Max…but not his…never his again. Tears bubble and spill.

"Lucy?"

I let one sob out and feel the heavy bed shake with me. I feel Jake's arms around me, pulling me up to him, crushing me against his strong chest. *But not his…never his again.*

I wail. I cry. I scream. It's not enough. All into his chest. My lips vibrate against his shirt.

"No! She's fine…just leave us…go." I hear Jake's commanding voice through my long tormented cries.

I don't stop. I lift my arms, my fingers claws, grabbing at his shirt, holding on. Screaming.

My throat betrays me, gives up. I keep crying. I keep screaming. I don't have sound to my wails, just wet sobs and rasping breaths. I keep screaming. One long, continuous wail. One shuddering, shattering cry.

I feel Jake's arms pushing me back against the pillows again, but he doesn't let go. I feel his hands pull at mine, taking them off his chest and laying them on my lap, but he doesn't let go. I feel his warmth, his strength. I cling to it.

…but not his…never his again.

I shake and whimper, soundless, tearless, my body too weak to give strength to my pain.

"Be a good girl…Get some sleep now, Lucy." I keep my eyes closed. I listen to his soothing sounds. I cling to Jake's voice… *And I pretend it's his.*

37 Her

My eyes are open before I realize I'm awake. I cough a little and become more aware of everything.

I'm alone. The room is darker. I can see the cup with straw and I reach for it, pulling painfully at an IV in my hand, but I can get it.

My head hurts, my side hurts, my wrist hurts, my throat hurts.

My heart hurts.

I start to cry again, a calmer, deeper cry.

Max. Why did you leave me?! Why?!

I can't get the sounds out of my head. No matter how loud I sniffle and cry. I hear the sounds of the accident. Bangs, metal scraping, screaming.

I'm startled to hear the door open. I try to sniffle and sit up more.

Jake's at my side quickly. I try to smile at his deep frown. *I try not to compare it...*

He brushes my hair back off my forehead and holds the cup for me to sip more. I watch him walk away and get more water from a plastic pitcher and bring it back to me.

I take another big sip before pushing it away. "Is...is he really...?" I'm not brave enough to finish.

Jake only nods. He's not brave enough to answer out loud.

He holds me while I cry more silent tears, my body lifeless, save the regular pulls of deep breaths in to carry more tears out. I feel his tears soak my hair.

38 Her

A nurse interrupts us. Our tears long spent, we've been quietly holding each other. Jake doesn't let me go. I hold onto his arms still.

"I'm sorry…I just need to get a few vitals…"

Jake kisses my head and starts to move, I cling harder to his arms. He whispers, "I'm not going anywhere." I let him move to stand at the end of my bed. I let the nurse take my temperature and blood pressure. I'm a limp rag doll. I even have rag doll eyes, big and unblinking, and a rag doll mouth, closed and small.

When she leaves with an apologetic smile to Jake, he moves to take my hand again and I cling to him once more.

"Dad's outside. He's called your parent's already. He has them on a plane for here tomorrow morning…" I nod.

I swallow, but my voice hurts to speak. "Where's Alex?"

Jake just shakes his head. "Dad didn't think it was good for her to be here..." He doesn't need to say that she's somewhere in a bed crying too, unable to make sense of all of this. Big balled up tears fill my vision and fall hard down my cheeks, bouncing to our hands.

"Tell me...how..." *I don't want to know....I've tried to pretend that this is a nightmare.* But the efficient nurses and doctors coming and going don't let my fantasies take hold. I've tried to push away the sounds in my head, but they drown out everything else. *I need to know. I have to know what happened to my Max.* My breath catches at thinking his name, but I squeeze Jake's hand back harder.

He almost whispers, but I hear the raw edge of his throat, cutting against each word. "From what the police have told us...you were pulled over and...and another car behind you zipped around without stopping at a light." He swallows and I rub his fingers to help him to keep talking. *I need him to hurry. I don't know how strong my resolve to hear this is, but it's fading fast.* "A delivery truck had the right of way and turned straight into the car...pushing it into yours. You were luckily thrown out and the whole mess was pushed further down the sidewalk away from you. Max..." He stops, blinks and breathes for a second. "He didn't suffer, at all...that's what they told us. His side...shit...his side was hit hardest and he was crushed..." He can't continue. And I can't continue to listen. *Crushed...I don't ever want to hear that word again.*

I roll over and turn away from his description. He puts his hand on my shoulder and doesn't move, doesn't rub, doesn't squeeze. Just keeps his hand on me. A warm spot against the cold that grips my heart and stomach. I shake and cry quietly again. I hear him crying behind me too, but his hand never moves.

I don't hear the door open. I only feel Jake's hand pull away finally.

"Lucy, sweetie…" It's Ron. I roll over and have my arms out for his embrace. I hold him while the big man cries in my arms. His hug hurts my shoulder and rib, but I don't really feel the pain. I only feel his warm wet tears on my thin hospital gown. I look up and see Jake's tears and reach my hand out for his.

We've all lost so much… I'll never be anything but lost again.

39 Her

I haven't had the strength for what I've done today.
Being numb helped, but I don't know where I found the
strength to stop crying after each person came in. PJ and
Cathy. Laura. Jeff. Dan and Mike. Jake stayed in my room,
never leaving my side. That helped. Ron has taken care of
everything. That helped too.

He told me the driver is in critical condition with head
trauma. I don't even remember his name. Max only said that
Jeff was going to keep an eye on me for him from now on…
None of that matters now. I know Ron assured the driver's
family that all the bills will be paid and he'll have the best
care. Jeff told me. *I know Max would want that…*

I don't know how I've been able to think his name
without choking on my tears, but being numb has helped. I
haven't been able to say it out loud without a searing pain, a
spreading pain that tingles my fingertips, tries to push away
the numbness.

I am greedy for the numbness. I hold onto it tight.

I try not to say his name.

The doctor says I can go home. This shakes my hold on the numbness. *I can't go home. He isn't there. I can't.*

Jake sees my panic. "Shhh…your brother and his wife want you to go with them tonight…so they can take care of you…okay?" I nod. *I'd sleep anywhere except alone in our bed.* I lose it again. I roll away from everyone watching and cry softly again. Jake's hand stays on my shoulder. It's a reminder that I'm still here, still in this nightmare. But I'm not alone.

40 Her

The mind is a strange map. Mountains of memories forged and forgotten, fields of feelings formed and processed, rivers of functions automatic and learned. All connected. All divided. All equal. All nothing in comparison to the next.

I wake with the memory of pancakes on Sundays. That smell and sound of childish laughter mix and I'm taken back to the last day of summer before I had to start first grade. Mom yelling that breakfast is ready. PJ home for the weekend from college, rubbing my sleep-hair head and racing me down the stairs.

It's only a second, but for that second I forgot. *Max is gone. I'm lost. All I am now are memories.*

I hear the sound of PJ racing Priscilla and Cassie down their stairs. I pull myself up from Cilli's little bed. I have to pee. *Damn this body and its need to function.*

I quietly leave the bedroom and close the bathroom door. The girls' bathroom is bright pink, with lavender and ballerina's and princesses. It's sweet. And I can hardly see it through my tears again.

I don't know what I'll have to face today...Mom and Dad. Alex. I look at myself in the mirror. I take as deep a breath as my rib will allow and start to turn for the door.

I sit back down, hard. *Funeral arrangements. Ron will take care of everything. I know he already is. But I'll have to be there. I'll have to face it. Alone.*

I will have a hard time pretending Max is with me today...but I will try. My love, for you, I will try to be everything you expect of me. But I am weak and these tears are strong.

Why did you leave me...

41 *Her*

It is worse than I imagined. A sea of black. A churning, tossing, moving, arms pulling, lips kissing sea of black clothed mass. I lost sight of Max once, and I panicked, shoving a stranger out of the way. Jake pulled me to the side, so I could have a clearer view of the front of the room. He hasn't left my side except to check on his mom.

The casket is empty. Max's ashes are already in a small box. I'm not a fool. I don't think Max is here. In this room. But his picture is, at the front, surrounded by flowers. It was the one thing I insisted on. No white flowers. No reminder of our wedding, only six short months ago. I breathe quickly to control my tears.

Blink. It's Max's voice I hear. His voice has been with me…getting me through the worst of it. *I'm trying, Max.*

But I need to see his face. *To get through this…I need to see Max.* I keep saying his name over and over in my head. A mantra, a prayer, a beginning to a wail I will let loose when I am alone again.

I look down at myself, at the simple black dress I'm wearing. Mom picked this out for me. She and Dad went to our apartment and packed a small bag for me. I'm staying at Ron's and Alex's tonight. *It's closer to the...to this place. But I needed something black...to fit in with the sea of blackness.*

I lift my head and push my shoulders back. Max wouldn't like it if I lost control here. He would expect better of me. He'd want his wife to hold her head up. *Be strong.* He'd expect me to be gracious to the strangers surrounding me. Just like our wedding. Men and women I never met, all passing with whispered wishes for me. *You can do this, baby.*

I'm trying.

"Do you need to sit down?" Ron is at my side again. He's taking turns with Jake. *The strong Traeger men taking care of their own.* I shake my head. I still have a wrap on my ribs and wrist, a few bandages on my arms, legs and face, but I don't feel this pain. It's shadowed by the tear in my heart.

I do however have to pee. I remember this from the book Max made me read. Early pregnancy. "Please excuse me." I put my hand on my stomach and walk out the doors. I ignore the eyes all staring at me. Pity, curiosity, sympathy...I ignore all of it. I especially ignore the blatant appraisals. I frown at these stares. From men. Men I don't know or barely know. *It was the same as at our wedding...and I can't think of that right now.*

I smile at the nod I get from Jeff and his girlfriend, Anna. When he introduced me to her earlier, it was startling to see him with tears. I know he loved Max as more than an employer. He looked up to him, tried to be like him. Jeff blames himself for not driving that day... *But I'm glad he's safe at least...*

I almost hit Becca with the bathroom door. "I'm so sorry!" She stops and laughs, but stops herself quickly and grabs me in another hug. I hug her back, but quickly move into a stall. The human body is a machine. Like an ant, it can carry a load of emotions far heavier than its own weight. *But it still has to stop for the stupid stuff.*

When I come out to wash my hands, Becca and Stephie are still here, waiting for me.

Stephie breaks the silence, her bright, loud voice piercing in the small space. "You look great! I mean...you look like crap...but you're holding up great, Luce. You really...I wish I could take you out drinking from here." She's awkward when she's emotional. I've learned this about her. She usually acts brisk and offensive when she's uncomfortable.

Becca pushes her with her hips and smiles at me, "I know everyone's asked you this already...is there anything we can do? Anyway we can help?"

I smile too. It's a small smile, but genuine. Max's friends meant the world to him. *He'd be happy to know that they're here for me now.* I grab one of their hands in each of mine. "I'll let you know. For now, I'm just trying to hold it together, ya know?" I let go and brush away a stray tear. I've tried not to cry today.

I turn and look at myself in the mirror. *Max always told me how beautiful I am when I cry. He liked to make me cry*

*when he punished me...or when he was feeling in a rough
mood in bed.* I almost moan out loud at this thought. I look
down, embarrassed, in case Becca or Stephie saw my cheeks
flush, my breathing speed up. I splash cool water on my face.

"Well, you're doing great. Max would be proud of you,"
Becca understands a little. I talked to her earlier today. I told
her I was trying to live up to what Max would want from me. I
smile again at her reflection.

We leave together and I walk over to Mom and Dad.
They've been huddled with PJ, Cathy, and Laura. Dad and PJ
put their arms around me. I'm getting used to hiding behind a
curtain of a small smile and held breath. *Don't mind that
shriveling, sniveling, sobbing girl behind the curtain...I am
the Great and Powerful Widow who can grant any onlooker a
graceful smile. How silly a mind can be in a time of tragedy. I
picture myself green...I'd rather be riding away on a
broomstick and torturing some small villagers than having to
be here and going through this. I'd rather be home in Max's
arms for the rest of my life...*

"Lucy?"

I turn and see Tracy, Rich, Catherine and Kevin walking
towards me. My old friend, boss, and co-workers. I pause.
Max wouldn't like this. Wouldn't like them here. *But reality is
a bitch.* He's *not here.*

I put my arms around Tracy and cry-laugh against her
collar and red hair. I haven't seen her in almost five months.
*Not since...well...since that horrible night Max punished me
for letting Rich put his hand on me.*

I don't look at Rich though. I don't touch him. *I can't do that. I won't do that.*

Jake is next to me, out of nowhere. I hug Kevin and Catherine. Rich doesn't move towards me, but puts his hand out and lets it drop when I don't respond.

"You shouldn't be here." Jake's voice is hard, low, deep. *Max's words, Max's voice.* I glance up at him. *Max's look.*

Rich blinks at Jake, then turns to me and gives a small smile, before turning again to Tracy. Laura told me that they're seeing each other now. She broke up with Josh officially and is only dating Rich. *Good for them. Jake's right, they shouldn't be here. Not here, not now.*

I let Jake take my arm and pull me back towards my family. Laura smiles an apology and walks over to Tracy. I let Mom fuss over pushing my hair back. She tried to get me to pull my hair into a braid today. But I need the curtain to hide behind. I don't look up at Jake again. I just feel his tension next to me. He doesn't leave my side again.

I wake up in the middle of the night. This is a strange bedroom. Alex made the room nice, but I'm still scared for a moment. It takes some time to realize where I am. And why I'm here.

Nightmares fill my days and nights.

I roll over again, pressing my hand to my stomach. *Well, baby…just you and me now.* I'm out of tears. Or in shock still.

What are the stages of grief? Is shock one of them? Should be if it's not. I'm in shock by how much can change in a heartbeat.

It seems like only a heartbeat ago I was falling for Max. A heartbeat and I was forever changed by his views on relationships and me. A heartbeat and he slapped me for the first time. Beat…happily married. Beat…his brutal anger. Beat…back to happiness, hope, love. Beat…gone. *I want to live in a heartbeat. The one with us, together, happy to be us, to have a baby. I want that beat back! It's not fair!*

I slam my fists against the bed. I give into a real tantrum. I scream almost silently into the pillows. I thrash and hit and scream until I'm exhausted of tears again. *But I'll never be without tears anymore.*

I curl into a ball and hold my stomach. *It's going to be okay, baby. No, Max. It'll never be okay ever again. I'll never have your mouth, your body, your eyes on me again. I'll never have your love to protect me again. To keep me and our child safe…even from yourself.*

I know that's why you said that you wouldn't punish me. I deserved it. I deserved your anger. I should've been stronger. I know I trusted you, deep down…it's the only way I was able to stay…after everything you did. All the ways you hurt me. I know you would never really *have hurt me.*

I know you loved me. And I know I'll never be loved again. I'm lost and alone. I don't know if I can do this, Max. If I can be a mom alone to your child…please…please come back to me!

I cry again, fool's tears, and I fall asleep imagining Max next to me. *I know it'll hurt more when I wake up alone, but I don't care. I'll punish myself with my foolish dreams and wishes.*

42 Her

Jake opens the door for me. *Was it only ten days ago that he was here with me? When Max was so angry and waiting for us?*

I've avoided being here. I've stayed with PJ or Alex and Ron. I've not been able to face coming home to our empty apartment yet. But I knew I'd have to, eventually.

Mom and Dad will be here soon. I take a deep breath and walk slowly in. *Nothing's the same.*

I move quicker through the rooms into our bedroom. *Everything's cleaned and...*

"What...where's everything?!" I turn on Jake. He stays just outside the room, watching me. "Where is all of Max's stuff?"

"I had a cleaning crew come in yesterday. They boxed everything up for you."

"Why…? I don't want anything in boxes! Where are the boxes, Jake? Tell them to bring me everything now, here, now!" I'm hysterically yelling, loud and shrill. I hurt my own ears.

He just stands there, watching me, no answer. I turn and move around the room again. Into the closet. A few things are still here. A few shirts. I grab one and pull it to my face. I can still breathe in Max's musky-linen smell. I sit on the floor of the closet, holding the shirt against me.

I don't move, I don't cry, I just sniff and hold. I hear Jake walk away.

I stay in here, in the relative darkness. I lay down on the carpet, just like the night Max kept me here, safe from his anger. I put his shirt on over my dress, wrapping myself in him.

I must've closed my eyes and slept, because I didn't hear my folks arrive. I didn't hear Mom open the closet door more. I just feel her cool hand on my forehead, like when I was a kid with a cold. I let her pull me up and walk me out of the bedroom. But I wrap Max's shirt around me more. *I'm not taking it off. Ever again.*

Jake is still here. He and Dad are talking quietly at the table. I glare at him. *He had no right to take anything from here!* "Where are the boxes, Jake?"

"They're at the house. In Evanston. Nothing will happen to them, I promise. Everything's safe and there when you're ready to go through it."

"I want them back. Now." Mom tries to rub my arm, to soothe me. I shrug her hand off.

Jake only shakes his head, his look unreadable. "I left all the pictures, Lucy. I only had them take the things…the things I know won't help you right now." He looks at the shirt I'm wearing. "I'll have to complain that they forgot to check the laundry…"

I move quickly. I slap him. Hard. I try for as hard as Max ever slapped me. "Lucy!" Mom is grabbing my hand as I aim to slap him again. But Jake didn't move. His head only jerked a little at my feeble attempt to hurt him.

I pull my hand away from Mom, but it's Dad that stops me from yelling in his quiet, calm voice. "Lucy…you need to calm down, sweetheart. Jake did the right thing…I know it's hard to see that right now. But," he stands to hold me in his bear hug, "you're better off not having to do that yourself…go through everything here yourself right now." I shake with anger and grief in his arms.

I don't want to hear any of this. I push him off me and turn quickly back to the bedroom, slamming the door behind me. I crawl in bed and am grateful that the sheets weren't washed. I can still smell Max here too. I pull the covers over my head, wrapping myself around his pillow.

I've decided. I'm never getting out of this bed.

43 Her

"Are you sure you don't want us to stay longer, sweetie…we'd be happy to stay here. Or you could come home with us." Mom is still hugging me. I look at Dad behind her and roll my eyes.

"Come on, Lizzie. We're going to miss our flight." PJ hugs me one more time; Dad leans over and kisses my forehead. Mom finally lets go of her squeeze on my arm.

I quietly close the door. I take a deep breath before turning around though.

I haven't been alone in over five weeks. I thought I'd go crazy with having my folks here that whole time. PJ and Cathy and the kids were here a lot too. But I've been alone in bed at night.

I cried when Mom ripped the sheets off the bed and washed them. I wouldn't let her touch Max's shirts though. I've kept them near me.

I've managed to get out of bed a little each day, a little more each day at least. But I've walked through our home like a crazy person at night, pacing, thinking, unable to sleep, alone. I've expected Max to come find me and bring me back to bed most nights. I've almost convinced myself that he will some nights.

Turning now and looking around, I feel that same craziness take hold. I panic. *Calm down. Just breathe.* I still hear Max's words, but it's my voice now.

I've only left the apartment a few times and that was only this past week. I had to in order to convince Mom and Dad to leave finally. I couldn't take more of Mom's constant babying. *Okay. I've acted like a big baby, crying and not doing anything for myself. But I needed to get them out of here.*

Now I think I made a mistake. I don't want to be alone here. *It's too lonely being alone when Max should be here.*

I'd promised Mom that I would go for a walk today. It's starting to warm up outside again. But this thought only makes me realize that it hasn't even been a year since I met Max. And that thought is too much right now.

I pace, grabbing his shirt and wrapping it like a scarf around my neck, holding a sleeve under my nose. *This counts as walking.*

44 *Her*

"Get up." I open my eyes and have to blink sleep away after gasping. I thought it was Max standing over me for one too brief of a second.

"I really need to change our locks." But I sit up with my legs over the edge of the bed.

"You really need to get a shower and get ready." Jake throws my robe at me.

"What are you doing here, Jake?"

"I'm here to take you to the doctor appointment you missed." I glance at the alarm clock. *Shit. I did miss it.*

"I'll call and make a new one…go away." I start to lay back down.

He grabs my arm and yanks me up. "Jesus. Look at you! You're skin and bones, girl." I look down at myself. The waistband of my sweat shorts is tight, but everything else just hangs on me. I've tried to eat, but I haven't been able to get more than a few bites down each time. I've mostly slept since my folks left. I have to think…*that was a week ago?*

Jake stares at me a little longer, a deep frown on his face. I try to squirm out of his grip, but he only squeezes harder.

He pulls me towards the bathroom and shoves me through the door. "Take a quick shower. We're leaving in fifteen minutes."

His take charge attitude pisses me off. *He's not Max. I don't have to take orders from him!*

"No. I'm not going anywhere with you. Just get out of my house."

"I'm warning you, Lucy. Close the door and take a shower. Now!" His face is as angry and dark as Max's would be. I almost cry, but being angry is feeling too good. It's a break from despair.

"Warning me?" I laugh loudly in his face. I haven't even seen him in weeks. "Who the hell do you think you are?"

He speaks slowly, through gritted teeth. "If you don't start getting ready, girl, you're going to get the spanking you deserve."

I freeze. For one blink, I freeze. Then I'm lost in a flare of temper I've never felt before. It's an overwhelming surge of all the grief, pain, anger I've felt since losing Max.

"Fuck you, Jake!" I scream this in his face as loud as I can.

And he reaches with his long, strong arms, grabbing me and yanking me back out of the bathroom. I try to get away, scratching and pulling at his hand, kicking at him as he yanks me. He pushes me onto the bed, on my stomach and holds me down, swatting my butt with his hand, hard. Both cheeks get equal abuse. I'm screaming at him to get off me, to stop. Soon I'm screaming in pain too.

Jake doesn't stop. He just keeps hitting my sore butt, blistering me more with his hand, until I'm only crying in pain.

He finally stops, but still holds me down, a little breathless, "You ready to behave, Lucy?"

I only cry into my bed, refusing to answer him. He smacks my lower cheeks several more times, causing me to cry out, "Yes! Yes."

He doesn't move though, only breathes a little deeper, "If I let you up, you are going to go straight to the bathroom, clean yourself up and meet me at the door in fifteen minutes?"

I sniffle a little more, but quickly answer when I feel his hand lift off my butt again, "Yes!"

He moves his hands away, "Good girl. Hurry up."

And he leaves the room.

45 Her

And I do hurry. I don't stop to think; I just get ready quickly. I don't even look at myself in the mirror. I don't look at my butt. I just run around and fly out the door down the hall.

I don't look at Jake as he opens the door for me. I don't look at him on the elevator ride down. I don't look at him as he opens his car door for me. Or even when he gets in and drives away.

I look at my hands instead. I look at my rings.

Max would be very disappointed in me, that I missed the appointment. I meant to get up. I was even excited for today's visit. First ultrasound. But facing this alone was too much. I got in bed and tried to calm myself, rubbing my belly and telling baby that we'd be okay. *I don't believe this, but I hope the little bugger does.* I must've fallen asleep.

Mom went with me to the first prenatal visit. Dr. Patel was very kind, all of her staff were, offering condolences. I didn't have to go through that alone at least. Kindness is the worst. I have to smile and act sweet, when I really just want to cry and rage against the unfairness of life.

But today, I was going to be alone. I should've called Alex or Cathy or Laura, but I felt pathetic. My house is a mess. I haven't had the energy to do anything. I've hardly left the apartment since Mom and Dad left.

I blink in the sunlight, staring out the window at the streets passing quickly. "I don't think I can just walk in for an appointment that I'm two hours late for…" I say in a small voice.

Jake's voice is still gruff, but a little nicer, "I made a new one for you this afternoon."

I swallow, "So…how did you know I missed it?"

He grins at me, a rather wicked version of his usual boyishness, "I'm keeping tabs on you. I got a call saying you needed to reschedule."

"Oh." I feel only a small twinge of anger at the invasion of privacy. "I didn't think doctors were allowed to give out patient information."

He only grins again. I know that Dr. Patel is somehow a family friend. She never even blinked an eye when I'd show up with belt marks on my butt for appointments. I guess I shouldn't be surprised that she'd share information with Jake.

I turn my head again and stare out the window. I'm not angry; somehow, I feel a little better. I shift in my seat. *My butt doesn't. But I've had worse.*

46 Her

The goo is cold no matter what they said about warming it up. I strain to see the wand move across my little bump. I'm ashamed of the bones sticking out at my hips. Dr. Patel already lectured me on eating more.

Waiting for her to come back into the room for the ultrasound, I stared at the ceiling. My butt still tingled a little against the paper. I was shocked. *Jake spanking me...never would've seen that in my future. But then...I can't see my future anymore.* I knew that Jake only did what he thought Max would've done. He's tried to be supportive and protective. For Max.

Staring at the ceiling, I made a promise to myself, to Max, to our baby, that I was through with wallowing in self-pity, that I would take better care of myself for the sake our baby. That even though I only want to crawl in a dark hole and forget about life, I know that's not an option.

I have to keep our baby safe and healthy. I've done a bad job so far, but I promised to do better. For Max.

"Here we go…Lucy, meet your baby." Dr. Patel turns the screen more towards me, pressing down more with the wand. It takes me a minute, and her pointing, to make out the little bugger's shape, so tiny, so innocent. I cry and shake. But for the first in time in weeks, with only a small amount of pain.

"Can you…can you get Jake for me…to see?" Her assistant nods and leaves the room quickly.

When the door opens, Jake comes in quietly, looking a little awkwardly towards me on the bed. I'm covered except for my stomach, but he doesn't look at me.

Dr. Patel points at the screen, "Your niece or nephew wanted to say hi."

He leans into the screen, even putting his fingers over the tiny figure. "Hey there, little guy! It's good to see you!" He has tears in his eyes when he turns to smile at me. And then he winks.

I let out a laugh and a cry at the same time. I hiccup and the screen goes crazy moving around. Dr. Patel gets up and wipes my stomach off for me. She's already printing copies for me to share with my family.

47 Him

"I'm glad to see you have an appetite." I risk a finger reaching for a fry off her plate. Lucy's already wolfed down her burger and she's on her second vanilla shake.

She only smiles, rubbing ketchup off her lips with the back of her hand. We haven't really said much since leaving the doctor's office. I didn't ask if she wanted to eat; I just opened the door to the diner around the corner. I didn't ask what she wanted; I just ordered for us.

So I was surprised when she spoke up and got the waitress' attention to order a shake too.

She looks like shit. Her eyes are hollowed with dark circles, pale and she's way too thin. Dr. Patel said she wants to see her in one week and stressed in front of me that she needs to see some weight gain. I smile again. *Looks like that won't be a problem if I can get Lucy to keep eating like she is right now.*

She scrunches her nose at me in response to my smile. *It's a good look for her.* Almost puts color into her cheeks again.

I was shocked when I opened the door to the apartment earlier. It was a mess. Dishes everywhere, mostly uneaten food left on some of them. The TV left on, but quiet. Furniture turned over. The bedroom looked like a bomb had gone off, clothes and crap everywhere. And Lucy looking so lost, so fragile, broken.

I talked to Mom yesterday. She said she spoke to Lucy briefly the day before, but she didn't know really how she was doing. She wanted me to check on her today anyway. When I got the call from Dr. Patel's assistant, I was pissed. I didn't think, I just went to see Lucy, cancelling all my afternoon meetings and giving my appointments to my staff.

At the funeral, I'd told Lucy that I was going to keep an eye on her, that I'd made a promise to Max that I would watch over her. *Well...to his ghost I guess, but I still intend to keep my promise to my brother. I won't let anything happen to his wife or baby. Not if I can help it.*

Seeing the state Lucy was in, the state their place was in...spanking her was the least I was thinking about doing.

I haven't spanked anyone in a long time. The first girl was high school. Autumn. It was more fun and games then, nothing serious. She was my first everything. I loved watching her ass get red. I loved hearing her fake beg for me. I knew I wasn't really hurting her, that I wasn't really making her beg me to stop. I didn't care, it was good enough. I was getting laid.

When I got drunk one night and tried to spank her for real, she broke up with me. I didn't try it again with any other girlfriends until later in college. Similar results, plenty of play, but nothing serious. I never went far enough, never tested any commitments.

Instead, I tried for the more normal relationships. Like Julia. *Now that one was a mistake. That was a girl who didn't want to be a man's equal. She wanted to rule.*

I guess if I'm honest with myself, I've chosen to be with strong women, women who don't *need* me. Women who would slap a lawsuit on any guy who tried to spank them.

Women who would never be what I really want.

Not women like Lucy. I swallow. *No use going down that road. Not now. Not ever.*

But my hand still tingles thinking about Lucy's ass. I didn't get to see her cheeks turn red, didn't get to see my handprint on her. *But I have a pretty good imagination.*

I can't help smiling as I watch her chug her shake, then grab her forehead. "Brain freeze?"

She only nods, pressing both hands to her head. Her eyes are bright blue when they open again.

48 Her

I stop at my door. "I…I know you already saw…how bad it looks. But I'd rather you not come in again…okay?"

Jake nods, his deep frown in place again, "As long as you promise to clean up before I'm back tomorrow."

I nod and even give a small smile. I take the bag of groceries from him and open the door just a little to get in.

I'm keeping my promise, Max. I walk down the hall, taking in how messy everything really is. *Wow…you really let yourself go, baby.* I smile thinking that wouldn't quite be the words Max would have for me if he ever came home to find our place like it is now.

And the fact that I can smile instead of cry makes me almost cry anyway. *No. No more tears today. Okay…not until I'm in bed again later at least. Deal? Deal.*

I put the groceries away. I sigh before tackling anything more though. *Maybe I need some motivation.*

I pick up the phone. Luckily Laura picks up on the second ring; I was just about to lose my nerve and hang up. "Hey. Wanna come over later?"

"Hey yourself! I'd love to. I should get out of here around 5:30ish today. Want me to pick up something on my way?"

"No. I'll make us something to eat. See you then." I hang up looking around again. *Damn, that only gives me two hours. Yep, that's motivating.*

"Lucy, you've been holding out on me." Laura is laughing, wiping her plate clean with the last chunk of bread. "This was amazing. I wanted to stop, but I just couldn't…you've added thirty minutes to my workout tomorrow with this shit."

I laugh, "Thank you." On my list for tomorrow is heading to the gym. I'm going to start jogging again. I'll go slow, but I want to get back to the point that I could follow in Max's footsteps. *It seems important somehow to continue some of the things he wanted me to do.*

Like the list. I'm not going to write one down, but I am making a mental list of chores for myself. I smile taking Laura's plate and mine to the kitchen. She follows with everything else from the table.

I managed to get the majority of the house clean. At least the areas she'd see. I'll work on the rest tomorrow.

And I frown just as I start to smile again. I was thinking about Jake saying he was coming here tomorrow. *Thinking about him spanking me earlier today. Be honest. I was thinking about him spanking me* tomorrow *if I didn't have the place clean. And...how tempting it is to leave it a little dirty...* I shake this thought off.

I look at my fridge. Baby Traeger's first photo is on display. I touch it as I open the door. Laura gushed over it for the first half hour she was here, then I put it back on the fridge. Another one is propped up next to my bed. *In front of Max's urn.* I catch my breath thinking this, but shake my head to stop the tears.

"So...dessert?"

"Are you kidding me, stop demon woman!" But she's already pulling out two plates and forks. I pull the brownies out of the oven where I kept them warm.

We each take one then laugh at each other, reaching for another one. I lead us into the living room. Max never liked to eat on the sofa. *It was a rule.* I hesitate at the table, looking from it to the sofa and back again.

I slowly walk over to the coffee table and put my plate down. Laura doesn't notice or at least doesn't say anything about my uncertainty. She plops down next to me and digs in with her fork. I don't touch my plate, suddenly a little nauseous.

"You okay?" Her concerned look makes me smile.

"Yeah…just baby doesn't think there's more room right now." I pat my stomach.

"So your due date's in January?" I nod, taking another sip of water to fight back the rest of my uneasy stomach. "That means you have all summer to be at the beach, sportin a big belly and two piece…" She nudges my leg with her foot.

"*You* are a brat. I will look fabulous in a full muumuu thankyouverymuch." Thinking about summer doesn't make me happy though. I'd looked forward to celebrating our first date, our first kiss, our first everything.

Now I have another first…first summer without Max.

"I'm sorry…I seem to keep saying all the wrong things." Laura puts her plate down and holds my hand again.

I shake my head and wipe my eyes, not letting the tears fall. "No. I'm okay. I just have to keep getting out of my own head, ya know." Laura smiles and nods. "Thanks for coming over tonight. I really needed the company."

"I was hoping you'd return my calls sooner… I know your folks left last week… What have you been up to?"

I laugh. "Nothing. Absolutely nothing." I pick up my plate, but I still can't get myself to eat. Not on the sofa anyway. This actually makes me smile again. *I'm still Max's good girl.* I put the plate back down. Laura just watches and leaves her plate on the table too.

"So… What *are* you going to do?"

"Well, to be honest…I haven't even thought about it." I look a little embarrassed at her. "I don't really *need* to work."

Ron took care of everything. He came by a few weeks ago with all sorts of paperwork for me to sign. It was a whole bunch of life insurance, annuities, funds, accounts, properties, investments…it was more than I ever knew existed.

My head was spinning and my wrist was hurting, still healing from the accident. He didn't give me a final number, just said that when I was ready to go over everything in more detail, he'd have the firm's accountant meet with me. I only really remember hearing that the apartment was paid off. And that he'd keep a small sum in a checking account for me to use as day to day until I was ready to do anything else. And that all bills are paid automatically through a different account.

It wasn't much of a relief at the time. I remember my dad looking impressed. Mom looked stunned.

But now I can see that not having to worry about anything financial has been a huge burden lifted from my already overburdened shoulders. Seeing the look on Laura's face, I feel embarrassed by the wealth Max left me. *But I'd trade everything just to have him back…even for only a moment.*

Laura sees the shift in my look and quickly interrupts my thoughts. "Well…that's good news then. But ya can't sit around here, cooking like this and getting fat!" She nudges me again with a big smile. "Except of course, you will get large with child." She puts her hands straight out and blows up her cheeks.

"I thought I told you never to use that phrase again!" I throw a pillow at her face, laughing.

I'm looking forward to feeling our baby move, to seeing our child's face on another ultrasound, to watching fingers and toes grow. *For having our baby. Scared beyond belief, but looking forward to it. It means Max will always be with me, through our baby.*

"What about coming back to work for Cruela? She'd love to have you."

"Oh, God. No. No, thank you." I did actually think about it while I was cleaning earlier. I have a need to stay busy, at least until the baby is here. "Besides, I don't think I'll work once I have the baby...so I need to find somewhere to work that doesn't mind a short short-term employee."

"Well, since you don't need the money...what about charity work?"

"I was thinking the same thing. Maybe something with the symphony? ...Max loved the symphony." This thought does tug at my brow, but I smile and shake off the frown.

"Ooh...we could get all dressed up together and go to the opening night! Maybe I'd find a prince charming type in a tux. Yep, *that's* where you need to volunteer."

"For you, dahrling, anything."

I change the subject. She seems to understand that I need more distractions. I don't want to talk about me or anything to do with me right now. Laura fills me in on office gossip and happenings. Rich and Tracy are apparently very much in love now. Or he is anyway.

"So...you still haven't returned Tracy's calls?"

I shake my head, it's one of the things I've debated. "I…I know this may sound dumb. But Max wouldn't like it if I did…and…and I need to feel like I'm still…" I shrug.

She takes my hand again. "I get it. I do." She smiles until I finally smile back. "Besides, it's been so long…I know Tracy can be a big pain in the ass. She understands though. She was never a fan of Max's. Now, well…she gets why you wouldn't want to be around her just yet." This does make me smile. Maybe I'll pick up our friendship again, but I don't think so. I realized after all that happened that Tracy wasn't the type of friend I need in my life.

I need more friends like Laura, the faithful and devoted kind. I could use more friends that are willing to look you in the eye and ask the hard questions, but have faith in your answers too, have faith that you can figure things out for yourself, without judgment.

The rest of our night is spent with stories of bad dates. One after the other. Poor Laura has been out with every version of loser it seems. I laugh, but in the back of my mind, I think how scared I am. I'm nowhere near thinking about dating, but if I ever was… *I know no one will ever compare to Max.*

49 Him

I called her three hours ago. It only went to voicemail, with no call back. I was disappointed to not talk to her. Even more disappointed after not hearing back from her. Now, in the elevator, I'm getting angry. *Lucy better not still be in bed!*

I get to her door and open it with my card. I smile…*she didn't change the lock at least.*

Walking in, I can tell right away that she cleaned. It smells like oranges and blossoms…like her, clean and fresh and sweet.

I head into the kitchen. "Lucy." I look and see the bedroom door is open. I don't go in. I just put the bag of food I brought on the counter. I smile seeing how clean everything is.

Good. She listened to that part at least. Let's hope she's not still lounging around in sweats, crying all day. I frown. *Not that I can blame the girl. I had to stop my own faucets from running on more than one day lately. I still can't believe Max is gone.*

I stop. I don't hear anything. *Maybe she's in the bathroom?* I move towards the bedroom door. "Lucy?"

No response. I poke my head into the bedroom. It's clean too. But no Lucy. I spot the urn and the ultrasound picture. I feel my stomach flip-flop. The bathroom door is open.

Get ahold of yourself! She's not here is all. She's fine.

But I feel a stab of guilt. *Max must have felt like this when he came home to find her not here...she was at my place, waiting for me. Shit. This is all wrong. Max should be here and I shouldn't be.*

I turn to walk out. *I'll leave her a message later.*

I reach the front door just as Lucy comes in. She's beautiful with a jolt of fear before smiling in surprise at seeing me. Her cheeks flushs, hair wild from the wind. "You're early."

I can see her arms are full with groceries and bags. I grab two of the heavier looking ones and take them into the kitchen for her. Lucy stops in the hall and tosses the shopping bags into the bedroom before following me.

I keep my back to her. I don't want her to see my reaction at seeing her walk in the door. I'm as hard as I was yesterday after spanking her. I'd hurried out of the room then too.

"You went shopping?" I try to keep my voice from sounding strained.

"Oh…yeah…" I glance at her as she puts her groceries on the counter. She looks a little embarrassed. "I had to get some new stuff." She pats her stomach. "I'm planning to overfeed this critter the next few days." She laughs at herself.

I'm under control again. I turn and laugh with her, "Good. I'll be glad to see it."

She turns to face me, fully. Her face isn't sad, but she's not really smiling either. "I want to say thanks…for yesterday. I needed…" she stops and her look frowns and turns…*coy*? "…a good *kick* in the butt." I watch her mouth as she says this. It's playful, stressing the word, toying with me.

I grin, "Anytime." She blushes, with that way she has, so easily. Max told me once that it was her expressiveness, her little responses and blushes that made him fall in love with her so fast and hard. *I can see why.*

I stop smiling and turn away quickly again. "So…what's all this?" I nod toward the spread of food she has on the counter.

"I'm making you a home cooked meal tonight." Lucy glances at the bag I brought, her eyebrow hooked in accusation.

"You don't have to do that…" But my stomach betrays me, growling. I rarely cook for myself. Usually the spaghetti variety is the most I do.

She laughs and pokes me in the rib. "How bout you help? You can chop onions…I think I've cried enough lately…"

I give her a small, soft smile. *I think so too.*

"Mom is going to be jealous. I'm not telling her that you've now outdone her with chicken parm..." I'm on my third helping. I'm happy to see that Lucy's had two herself. She was serious about eating well.

"I won't tell." She raises her fork in salute. "This was one of Max's favorites…" She has the faraway look again. She's gone quiet and solemn a few times tonight. I haven't interrupted. She needs to learn to get herself out of her head, to allow herself time to feel everything too if she needs.

She shakes her head and I'm rewarded for my patience with one of her prettiest smiles, big and lots of teeth. "Would you like more wine?" She's already reaching for the bottle. I shake my head. She only had water, but she insisted I have some Chianti.

It's funny. When I compare tonight to so many nights I had with Julia…or any girlfriend for that matter. I know Lucy is different. She's naturally submissive. She's naturally attentive and giving, feminine. Not like the women I've dated.

I recognized this in Lucy before. The first night I met her, she was obviously scared…and just so damn cute. So damn submissive…subservient. Her every movement was done to please my brother. I still feel a pang of jealousy thinking about that night. And guilt.

I talked to Max about Lucy's nature, after I broke up with Julia. The night I threw myself a housewarming party for my new building. Lucy fell asleep on the sofa. Max and I finished drinks and cigars on the roof.

I asked why he was so hard on her, why he had to demand so much from her. I was really trying to be her friend, to help him to see what she'd been telling me, about her fears. *But, hell, I was drunk. I wanted to know how he was able to get her do what he wanted...so easily.*

He said he couldn't help how he was with her, that she brought out the most primal needs to possess, rule, protect in him. His words. I laughed then, really drunk. *But I dreamt that night...well, I don't really remember much but a bare skin rug and beating my chest like an apeman, taking Lucy wildly.* I woke up soaked in sweat and guilt, painfully hard.

Max also said that Lucy didn't know herself before he met her. She didn't know her true nature really, that he brought it out in her too. *He was very poetic in his drunkenness that night. That she was a flower waiting to be de-thorned or some bullshit like that.* Max said that Lucy only pretended to be a modern girl, that she was really old-fashioned, that she really understood her place was next to her man. I remember gritting my teeth when he said, *under* her man. I don't remember what I said. I only remember how I felt. *Jealous.*

Watching her now, I know Max was right. *Lucy's true nature is submissive...she does everything to please everyone else.*

She interrupts my thoughts. "So Alex asked if I'd come up to the lake house next weekend..."

"I know. I suggested it. The weather's getting nicer. I think the fresh air would do you good." I shift uncomfortably, trying to keep my voice light. *I'm going to give myself permanent damage if I keep getting this hard around her*. "I can drive you up if you'd like…"

"I…I'm thinking I might be busy…" She smiles a little more.

"Busy?" I frown. *I hope she doesn't mean hanging around here, wallowing in grief more.*

"Maybe… I'm going to see about working at the symphony or a museum or something."

And I'm shocked at the stab to my stomach. I can't even think where it comes from for a moment. "You…you want to go back to work?"

She laughs. "Well…not work as in get paid, but volunteer maybe…if I can find somewhere that'll have me." I watch as she picks up the plates and walks away.

I watch her body move. She's too skinny. Her skirt stretches at the top, but her legs and arms look too thin. That doesn't stop me from watching her hips sway. Her little toes almost point with her barefoot steps; her hair is still crazy with frizz and curls, bouncing.

Shit, get ahold of yourself!

I don't move. She clears the table, smiling at me. I can't get up just yet. *Again.*

When she's in the kitchen, I bolt for the bathroom.

I close the door and breathe. *Just breathe.*

I look in the mirror. And just like that, I'm deflated. I can see Max staring at me. We were always told we looked more like twins than brothers with three years between us. No matter what else I think tonight, no matter what else I've thought over the last months…*I can't betray my brother. Not now. Not ever.*

I open the door slowly. I'm in control of myself again. *And for the last time.* I make this promise, knowing it's useless. *I can't control everything.* I grin. *It's not my fault your wife is my dream fuck, brother.* But I don't laugh. I feel only sadness that Max can't be here. For her, for me.

I sit back at the table and watch as Lucy brings two cups of coffee and brownies out.

I frown at her cup. She laughs, "Dr. Patel says just a little caffeine won't hurt me or the baby."

I put my hand over her cup. "Not on my watch."

She frowns again, but she lets go of the handle. I smile. I don't get hard; I'm concentrating really hard not to. *Her easy submissive responses though make it…* I clench my fist under the table…*damn difficult!*

"So…why volunteer?" I have to choke back the edge to my voice. She's still frowning, but answers with the same smile.

"I just need to keep busy…until the baby…" She's held her hand over her stomach a lot tonight, a sweet unconscious gesture. *Max's baby is already very loved.*

"Oh…well…if it's just to keep busy…" I shout at myself to shut up. I ignore that side of my brain. "…you could help me?"

She laughs and puts her soft, little fingers on my arm. "What could I do for you?" I watch her fingers curl around, barely covering my arm. *She's so tiny.* I notice her ring and pull my arm back. *Stop. Right now. Fucking stop this shit.*

But I'm still not listening... "You could be my temporary office manager...just until..." I shrug and look at her stomach. I'm already down this road. I take a deep breath, letting it out with a strong sigh. "I lost my office manager last month. I've been interviewing, but I haven't found anyone that'll work. My admin's been filling in, but he's not really cut out for it." *This is true. I could use the help. Stop kidding yourself. You don't want Lucy's help. You want her near. You want her* not *somewhere else.*

That was what stabbed my stomach. *The thought of her out there... in the world... around other people. Away from me.*

I'm as demented as Max.

I shake my head and start to retract what I just said, "I think volunteering would be go..."

"I'll do it!" She claps her hands. "Thank you, Jake. I know you're just being nice...but this is exactly what I need." Her eyes fill with crystal blue water, deep pools of unshed tears that magnify the color of her eyes. *Now who's being poetic?* "I just need to keep myself busy, ya know?" She wipes her eyes, but I watch one stray tear fall across her cheek, running towards her mouth. *I'd like to follow it with my tongue.*

I hear myself agreeing. I hear myself laughing with her. I hear myself saying that we'll work out the details. *Shit. Why can't I shut up already?*

"And I can help you interview for a replacement," she puts her hand on her stomach again, "when the time's right..." I nod. I should be backtracking, getting myself out of this deal, but instead...I nod. *Idiot*!

50 Her

I'm shaking. It's been a long time since I've worked really. And I've only had a few jobs before this. High school, I worked in a friend's dad's dental office; college, I worked as the front desk in admissions; and right out of college, I worked as a technical recruiter for a small talent placement company. The longest I worked anywhere was with the accounting firm, recruiting non-accounting positions. I loved it. I was even good at it. But it feels like a lifetime ago that I was around professional-types.

Max didn't believe in letting me work. I ignore this thought. *It's not going to help me. I need to focus on getting through today. That's all. I can't let Jake down. He's doing this for me. I have to do my best.*

I know this is good for me. I've been able to think of nothing else all morning. Almost. A miracle. I rushed through getting ready and eating a big breakfast.

I smile and jolt with a pothole. But I keep my breakfast down. I have a tight small smile for Jeff as I get out. I know he'll be back to pick me up. He's still on the payroll is how Ron put it. I know Jeff thinks it's his job to keep a close eye on me. For Max. *I like it…I feel connected still to my life with Max this way.*

Jake's still in his old offices, just outside the Loop. I look at my watch. *I'm early. Max's training. Never be late. A golden rule.* I smile. *He might not be pleased that I'm doing this, but at least I'm not breaking any of his other rules.*

I smooth my light dress down, pull my lightweight sweater away from my stomach and walk through the open doors. The offices are up a flight of stairs. I have to search for the door down the hall. I've only been here once, several months ago.

I finally find the door, but it's locked. The hallway is dark too. *I'm a little too punctual.* I wait near the only window in the area. I can see people walking quickly just a floor below on the street, cars slowing and speeding.

I'm saddened by the obvious tick of time. *This is why I need to stay busy…to avoid thinking about life and time and all that can happen and has happened and all that…*

"Hello."

"Shi…!" I jump and turn, startled by the clear voice in the hall behind me.

"Hey…sorry…didn't mean to scare you…" A dark-haired, dark-eyed man in baggy dark jeans, t-shirt, and multi-colored shoes comes a little closer. His smile is friendly though. He keeps one hand on his side and one on the strap to his bag slung across his shoulder.

"Oh. No…I just didn't hear you…" I try to sound more confident again. I'm still shaking though. Between being scared and running down the rabbit hole of depression again, I'm definitely shaken.

He smiles wider. "Are you waiting for Jake?" I nod. "Well, I'm Tim. One of his architects. I can let you in to wait inside…"

I smile too, "Thank you."

I follow him in and he turns on lights as we go. The place is a little different. The lobby and front desk is pushed forward more, there are more cubicles everywhere. Tubes of papers, long tables of reams of paper, every work surface is covered in papers. I follow Tim into a break area. He keeps looking at me from the side as he makes a fresh pot of coffee. The smell is intoxicating. I'm used to having one cup each morning, another of Max's rules. Going cold turkey with even this small addiction has been hard.

I step back out into the open area, looking around. I don't know where Jake's office is anymore. The space is jammed pack with tables and walls and papers.

I turn to see Tim smiling again at me. "So…are you a new client or a new architect?"

"Neither…I'm just here to help out. New office staff." I don't know why I shy away from saying 'manager' but it doesn't feel right. *I won't be here that long anyway*.

"Ah. Finally." I move out of his way as he walks back towards the front. I still follow him though, through the maze of stuff. "This is me. In case you ever have a question or need anything." He drops his bag at a cubby near a side window. I look around the space. It's a mess. A creative mess, but still an overwhelming display of objects, art, trinkets, and more papers. He moves a pile of rolled up blueprints off to the side and turns on his computer.

"Thanks." I think my first question would be how he gets any work done in all this.

"What's your name?"

"Oh…sorry." I put out my hand. "Lucy. Nice to meet you, Tim."

He takes my hand and wraps his other hand around both of ours. "You have a pretty smile, Lucy. I can say that…since you haven't officially started yet." And he winks at me.

I catch my breath. I lean against the makeshift wall between the cubicles and feel the tears spring up, but I look down quickly.

"Damn…I didn't think anybody blushed anymore!" He lets go of my hand. I pull away, moving back a few steps from him.

I try to smile, to not cry. I don't look at him. I look everywhere but at him. I know he was only joking with me, but…*the wink*! I hear a few more people coming in and I take the opportunity to walk away quickly. *I'll wait at the front.*

I bump into Jake's strong chest rushing to get down the corridor of cubes.

"Hey." He puts his arms around me and I feel even colder, more shaken. *I shouldn't be here. This was a bad idea.* "Lucy…you okay?" His deep, concerned voice, his spicy sweet smell, like vanilla and nutmeg, warm and inviting, his eyes. *All wrong.*

I push away. "I'm fine…I just need the bathroom." *That's true. My bladder is becoming the size of a pea with this baby. Maybe I'll just keep walking though. I can explain later that I changed my mind. Jake will just have to understand.*

But Jake grabs my chin and pulls my face up to his. *And I know. Right there. I can lie to myself all I want. But I know.* "Don't lie to me, girl."

I shake my head, "I just got a little overwhelmed…being here…all these people I don't know..." My eyes dart around. A few people are looking our way now.

He lets go of my chin and grunts a little, "That's understandable." Then he grins, his dirty-secret grin, "Besides…I know you wanna impress the boss." And I laugh watching his eyebrows wiggle. He can always make me laugh, even when my stomach hurts.

"I really do have to…" I gesture with my head towards the hall.

"Oh. Down the hall, first on the right." As I walk away though, he adds with a stern voice, "I'll be waiting right here, Lucy."

I guess I won't *be walking away.*

And I know that I don't want to…I like the idea of being here…near Jake.

51 Him

I watch her walk down the hall. I don't care that everyone's staring at me, smiling or frowning. I only have eyes on Lucy. Her dress isn't helping. It's sweet, but I can see her ass moving under the light material. *It looks like she doesn't have on...* I stop myself before I finish the thought. I rub my chin with both hands and stare up at the ceiling.

She looked like she'd seen a ghost. She was that pale, that scared. I just want to pick her up and carry her away from whatever had her so scared.

I'm absorbed in my thoughts; I don't notice Mitch until he shoves my coffee cup under my nose. "Hey, Jake. What's this I hear about you kissing somebody in the lobby?"

I groan and shoot him a look that instantly has him shutting up. Lucy returns, but stops a few feet away seeing my angry look. I give Mitch one last warning glare, before turning my attention back to her. I put my hand out and she does her little hip-rolling walk over to me, putting her small fingers in the center of my palm. "Lucy, this is my assistant, Mitch. He'll show you around today, get you settled in." She nods and smiles at him, pulling her hand away from mine and shaking his.

And for a brief moment I think about grabbing her arm and yanking her back against me. I smile, thinking about the office gossip that would start. *I'm glad that I'll be busy with client meetings all morning...I really need to keep a distance from her.*

Why'd you hire her then, jackass?

...But I know the truth. I can lie to myself all I want. I can pretend. But I know.

I like having her here...I like knowing that she's near.

52 Her

"What are you still doing here?" I jump at hearing Jake's loud and angry voice at the entrance to my little cubicle.

"Holy...! Jake, you scared me."

"I asked you a question." His eyes narrow and his body seems to fill the space more.

"I...I had a few things I wanted to finish before leaving." I saw him an hour ago and he said bye, so I thought he'd left already. *I don't know why he's so upset.* I glance at my watch. *It's only 6:00 p.m.*

"Jeff is waiting downstairs for you." It's an accusation, a pretty angry one at that.

This only ticks me off, like he thinks I'd leave Jeff just waiting. "I texted him. Told him I'd be down at 6:30 today."

"You leave at 5:00, Lucy." I've only been here a week. But on the first day, Jake came into my cubby at exactly 5:00 and told me to leave for the day. I was embarrassed then because Mitch and I were in the middle of a report. I didn't argue, I just quietly left, not making eye contact with Mitch or Jake again.

"I can decide for myself when to leave, Jake. It's not like you're paying me overtime…" I try to smile at this, to change the tension. It backfires.

He only gets angrier with me, his face hardening. "Don't get cute with me, girl. Get up. Now."

I flush at this, an angry, embarrassed flush. No one else is around at least. "What's the big deal, Jake…so I stay a little later tonight? I'm trying to help you."

He moves to stand next to me, swiveling my chair to face him and pushing it back quickly with both hands on the top, his forearms on the sides of my head. I have a moment of dizzying motion and intoxicating vanilla spice. "The big deal is I *told* you to go home at 5:00. So that's what time you'll go. No questions."

I try to push against his chest, to get him off. It's like a butterfly pushing a door. *Not gonna budge*. He grins and pushes my chair back even further. I'm afraid we'll tip over; I stop pushing and just stare up at him.

He hasn't been this close to me all week. If anything, he's avoided being near me or alone with me every day. We went to lunch that first day, but he invited a few people along and sat on the other end of the table.

Feeling his heat, his breath on my face, seeing his strength…I flush again. It takes any thoughts I had and twists them around to only one. *I want to run my tongue over the light hair on his arms.*

I lower my eyes and put my hands in my lap. *Get control of your damn prego hormones!*

53 Him

Heading out the door, I spot Jeff leaning against the car in the side alley. I frown, walking over. "Where's Lucy?"

He nods and takes out an earbud, I can hear the game he was listening to, "She'll be down soon." I frown more at this.

"She'll be down now." I turn to walk back into the building, but stop and walk back to Jeff. "From now on, if she's not down here at 5:00, you text me. Got it?" He nods again, but with a small smile. I ignore it and walk away quickly.

I told her to leave at 5:00 every day. She needs to rest. She's looking better, more like she should. Her eyes aren't as hollowed and I know she's been eating more, taking better care of herself. But she's also been working harder than I expected.

She's only been working for me for a week, but she's been a madwoman with organization. I almost don't recognize my offices. She arranged interior design interns to help archive all the plans and drawings that were lying around. And she came up with a new system with my project leaders for staying ahead of the piles, so in the future we won't have to deal with the same problem again, no matter how short staffed I might get.

I've been impressed.

Now, I'm just pissed. I stop at her cubicle and see her curls highlighted by the computer screen and her fingers pulling on her lips as she concentrates.

She jumps and I like seeing the little startled, big-eyed look for a moment. It doesn't take the edge off of my anger though.

I'm not thinking. I've been trying to avoid being close to her all week. But now, I'm too pissed off to think of this.

I shove her back, grinning at her shocked look again. I feel myself getting hard. But it's too late. I can't back down now. I push her even further back.

And her look changes, her eyes soften, lips part... *Stop! My imagination is going to drive me crazy*. I let her chair back up slowly.

"Now. Get your ass downstairs and go home."

She sits up straighter in the chair, chin up. "No. I have a few things I want to finish and I told Jeff I'd be down in a half hour. He can wait." I laugh at her effort to look commanding and determined. *Not very convincing on her*. Her eyes narrow more. "It's not nice to laugh at an employee, ya know."

"You're not an employee. But I *am* your boss. And I'll give you two more seconds to get your shit and get out of here." I cock my eyebrow at her.

"Or what?" She sits back and crosses her arms over her stomach. She thinks reminding me that she's pregnant will stop me from doing anything to her. *That's a mistake she won't make again.*

I answer her slowly, crossing my own arms. "Or I'll pick you up and carry you out of here. I don't care if you kick and scream, girl. You're going home when I tell you to." I grin at her even more determined look, almost a pretty pout now, "*I* won't be the one embarrassed."

She falters. I know she's imagining what everyone would see. *I am too. I like the image in my head.* She seems to think better of pushing me more.

She glares as she opens her drawer and slams it closed after getting her bag. She huffs as she stands up and stomps by me. Her cheeks are bright red, her lips squeezed tight over what she'd like to say to me. But I grab her arm before she's by me. "And I told Jeff to let me know if you're ever late meeting him again. I won't give you a choice a second time, Lucy." She looks like she's going to say what she's been thinking, so I cut her off, my voice a little deeper with emotion, "You need your rest. You're just starting to look healthy again…I don't want anything to happen to you."

Her mouth snaps shut and she looks down. I let her arm go and she walks out, but quietly. *Submissively.*

I on the other hand have to wait a minute to leave. *Wouldn't be good for the boss to be walking around with a hard-on in the office.*

54 Her

The first morning sunshine feels good, but the humidity is already climbing. I can feel sweat all over and not just from jogging. I slow to a fast walk. *Sorry, Max, won't make my numbers today*. I know it's more than feeling heavier and the heat. I've been pushing myself to get out of the funk I feel again. I woke up at 4:00 a.m. and couldn't go back to sleep. I came out for a run when it was still dark out.

I had a burst of energy the last few weeks, a happiness at working for Jake, feeling productive and needed again. I like most of the people there and I've had more than one person say I'm doing a good job. I smile thinking about the praises I've received from Jake.

I like when he pops his head into my cubby, just to smile and give me a compliment. I'm a puppy with a bone, wagging my tail in happiness all day afterwards. *Eager to please...that's me. But it's more than that. I like earning Jake's praise, his smiles. I like pleasing him.*

I feel a flutter in my stomach again at this thought. I've been having dreams of him lately. The boss bending me over every surface in the office and taking me from behind.

I keep blaming it on hormones, but I know that's not it. *Well, not all of it.*

I keep going back to the conversation we had…that night I was stuck in his elevator. But I never quite finish my thoughts. Because all thoughts always lead back to Max.

And I've been thinking a lot about Max this past week, about all of the firsts we missed celebrating so far this summer. First kiss, first date, first time he said he loved me. *That was today, Fourth of July.*

I've skipped over a lot of things this summer to avoid facing my pain with others around. I skipped Dan's birthday party. I skipped firm events that Ron and Alex invited me to. I've skipped going to their lake house. I haven't avoided them. I've seen my in-laws almost every week.

But I've avoided going places that remind me of Max, doing things that remind me of him. I've even stopped wearing my rings, at least in public. I've always felt a little self-conscious with such a large diamond. Somehow not having Max next to me, I feel a little strange with it on. Like it's a tag of possession, but I no longer belong to anyone. *Luggage lost at the airport that no one claims.* I'd rather not answer any questions about it when someone notices it.

In the privacy of my own home, I still cry myself to sleep some nights with pictures of him around me. I still wear his shirts around the house. I've bolted awake from a dream, thinking he was next to me and cried well into the morning hours.

I start to jog again. It helps with the anger. Tears I can handle now. I have some feeling of control over the sadness. I can keep it together around people for the most part. I only breakdown when I'm alone anymore.

I put my hands on my stomach as I pick up speed. Our baby helps with the sadness. I know I have to stay positive as much as I can for the baby's sake. *But the anger? I don't know what to do with it sometimes.*

And I've been dreading today. It was a turning point in our relationship. The "I love yous" were exchanged and I was forever Max's. *No choice. No control. Just his.*

Well…I still had the illusion of control for a little longer. I brush my cheek, shoving a tear away, thinking of that first slap. *When all illusions were cleared away. I had one last choice and I made it. Him. Always.*

Even with all of the doubts I had, that last day together. I said he couldn't change, but he was willing to try. For me. He said we'd have a fresh start. No matter the pain he caused me, his love was always stronger. Always.

He said I gave him everything he asked. At least that day, he knew I gave him the one thing I was afraid I couldn't. A child. And my belief in him. My faith in him. Always.

And now? It's been so long since I've felt his touch. His gentle pets or his rough demands. But I am still what he created, what he made me see in myself. I still need what he gave me. What only he could give me. Freedom to let go.

Freedom to give in. Freedom to submit. Freedom to love him unconditionally. Always.

What happens when "always" is cut short though?

I realize that I'm running too fast, my breathing isn't controlled. I slow down again and hear Max's training in my head. This helps. It helps with the anger and the sadness. I steady my pace and my breaths. *For Max. For our baby. I can get through anything. Even today.*

55 Him

I don't stand when the door opens. I just wait calmly at the table. I've been waiting for a while. I made myself coffee and toast while waiting for her. I know she's been jogging again. I asked Dr. Patel about it; she thought it was good idea.

I assumed that's where she was, but I still felt my heart leap a little when she didn't answer the door this morning. I still let myself in to look around here for her. I still called her cell. And I was still angry to hear it ringing from her bedside.

She jumps when she sees me. I haven't moved or said anything. "Shit, Jake. What are you doing here?"

"You left your phone!" I didn't mean to bark this at her, but seeing her now…my anger just jumps to the next level. She's wearing almost nothing, a tight tank and even tighter shorts. *Yeah, there's a tiny bump pushing out, but she looks like a model for a Goddamn sex ad, sweaty and beautiful.*

.

"What?" I pick up the phone I now have on the table and wave it at her. "So what? What are you doing here?"

"So what? You leave the house, dressed like that, without your phone, without telling anyone where you're going even?" I can hear how insane I sound. *I want to stop, really, I do.* But I can't seem to get an image out of my head. Of her being dragged off by some scary asshole and hurt. Because she was out alone, in the barely lit up morning…with no phone even to call for help. And looking like she does.

Lucy's speechless, shaking her hands in front of herself for a moment. A high frustrated sound of anger escapes her tiny throat. I watch as her face changes from shocked anger to full rage. "You have *no* right. *No* right to talk to me like this. And *no* right to just let yourself in here!" She marches back to the door and opens it. "Get out. Now!"

I don't move. My own anger has reached the rage level. But this only calms me. I've always been able to stay more level-headed when angry. My other emotions can briefly have control over me. But anger is the one emotion that somehow makes me more still, more focused.

I sit back in the chair and put one foot over my knee, a relaxed posture, my hands behind the top of my head. "I'm not going anywhere, girl."

And I watch her face change again. It's amazing how quickly her emotions flit across her face. Each feature morphing with the changes, it's almost dizzying watching her. She settles on a calmer show of anger. She slams the door closed and walks towards me.

And God help me. I'm stiff. I mean, full alert, this is gonna hurt later. Stiff.

Her hair swings and catches on her sweat soaked skin. Her nipples ache against the thin tank. Her legs stretch and tighten, hips roll and sway. She stops just in front of me, hands on her hips. This only makes her tits stand out more.

It takes everything I can manage not to take my eyes off of hers. I want to run my hands and eyes up and down every inch of her. *I want to watch her face change as quickly from this anger to one of pain.*

This thought rattles me a little. I drop my hands and look down, but bounce my eyes back up quickly. I'm glad I have my foot up. It's hiding how tight my shorts are now.

"So *what* did you let yourself into *my* house for, Jake?" She enunciates each word.

"I'll get to that." Her eyebrows raise and she looks like she's gearing up to yell again. I continue to speak calmly, but with a deep edge of anger. "First. Tell me what the hell you were thinking this morning. Jogging before it's light out, without your phone. And dressed like that."

She actually looks down at herself. I can see she's still angry, but my calmness is throwing her off. When she looks back up, there's an unexpected element of guilt in her face. Impossibly, I'm harder. I have to take a deep breath before speaking, but I can still hear the slight strain in my voice. I only hope she can't, "You weren't thinking, were you?"

She shakes her head slightly. But she still manages to sound a little defiant, a little bratty. "These are my running clothes, Jake. What am I supposed to wear? It's already hot outside."

I lower my eyes slowly, looking her up and down. I'm causing myself more discomfort, but I like seeing that it makes her uncomfortable too. She moves her hands from her hips and crosses them in front of her chest. I grin. "And I'm sure any guy who would come across you all alone in the dark wouldn't mind it at all." I let her look of guilt deepen. *As painful as it is to watch.* "Don't go out again in the dark for a run, Lucy. And never leave here without your phone, again."

She doesn't say anything, only looks down with her eyes, then lowering her chin.

I raise my voice and anger a little, liking how her head pops up, eyes wider, "Say it."

"Say what?" She blinks, a beautiful childish pout on her wet lips.

I grin only a little, slowly, "Yes, Sir."

She continues blinking. I try to read what her looks mean, but they change too fast. Finally, quietly, calmly, "Yes, Sir."

"Good. Now go shower. I'll make us some breakfast." Really, I just need her to walk away, so I can stand without her seeing the effect she has on me.

56 Her

I didn't argue when Jake told me why he came over this morning. I don't know if it's because he didn't really give me any room to argue or because of how I reacted to him earlier.

But I have plenty of time to figure it out this weekend now. I cross and uncross my fingers on my lap again.

Over breakfast he informed me that he was taking me to the lake house. That Ron and Alex were expecting us there early, so I needed to pack quickly. Or he'd do it for me.

Just like that. Bossy. Pushy. Commanding. So like Max.

But different too. I can't quite put my finger on it. *I responded to him. The same way I did to Max. I'm sorry, Max, but it's your fault. You made me aware of this need in me...to be dominated and controlled and commanded and...* I stop babbling to myself, to Max.

And that's what Jake did. I quickly glance at him. He looks straight ahead, not taking his eyes off the road, but I see his tiny grin. Smug. *He commanded and I obeyed.*

And I liked it. It felt comfortable, familiar. I take in a shaky breath and turn to look out the window, so he can't see the tears in my eyes suddenly.

Am I so desperate to feel Max again that I'll jump to obey anyone who shows the slightest dominance? Or is it because Jake reminds me so much of Max; and that he only acted that way because he's trying to act like Max for me? Thinking he's helping me?

It's not. It's only confusing me. I need to be thinking about my baby. And that's it. I cover my stomach again. I'm starting to really show. I've had to switch to some of the clothes I bought. I smile. All skirts and dresses still. Just what Max would've wanted to see.

But I'm going to be huge soon…I really don't need to be thinking about *any* guy. Especially Jake this way. *I had my love. Now I'll have our baby.*

I can forget my submissive side again. I can ignore it.

Now if I can just ignore the growing apprehension of going to the lake house. The last time I was here was with Max, for thanksgiving. I've been avoiding painful memories. And this weekend was already going to be bad.

Jake puts his hand over mine and I twist my head around to see him giving me his looking through me look again. He smiles though and squeezes my fingers just once. "It's going to be okay, Lucy. I promise."

I smile a little back. *Traeger men always keep their promises...I don't know how, but I know Jake will keep this one.* I take a deep breath and let it out slowly. *I'll be okay, Max. Your brother said so.*

57 Him

Mom and Dad aren't around when we arrive. A note on the counter says they went with the neighbors on the boat and would be back for lunch. I watch Lucy. She's moving around slowly, like she's never been here and she's trying to see everything.

I know her though. She's really trying not to see the past. "Let's unpack." She jumps at my voice. I grab our bags and head upstairs. She follows very slowly behind. I wait at the top of the stairs for her to catch up.

She looks like I'm walking her to the gallows. I walk past the room she usually shared with Max, the bigger room with the terrace. She pauses at the doorway and looks after me with a frown.

"You're small. You don't get the bigger room." I laugh at her confused look. But she follows me down the hall into the room I usually used. She stands just inside the door and

watches as I put her bag on the bed. "You'll stay here, Lucy."
I walk back to her and tap her nose with my finger, "New
room, new memories, girl." She nods and waits till I've
walked away a little before going further into the room. I can
see her moving around slowly and I see her smile a little too.

"Oh my God, remember that awful sweater you bought
him? He hated that scratchy thing and tried to throw it away."
I'm laughing too hard at the memory of Max with the
oversized sweater that felt like it had needles in it. Dad laughs
and nods. Mom puts her hands over her mouth, laughing hard.
I turn to Lucy; she's sitting on the sofa with her legs tucked
under a blanket. I'm sitting on the floor below her. "He threw
it away, but Dad found it the next day and made him wear
it...*with* the night before's spaghetti stains on it. It was...I
dunno...80 degrees out. And he had to wear that damn thing
all morning doing chores..." She's laughing so hard, she
suddenly jumps up, again, and runs to the bathroom.

She comes back, "Sorry. I think my bladder has either
shrunk to nothing or *it's* what's actually growing inside me."
She pats her belly. We all smile at her. *She really does glow.*
More than from the firelight. She's been laughing all day,
more than I've heard her in a long time.

We've been looking at photo albums and telling stories
of Max all day for her. She and Mom have both hugged and
cried a lot too. But for most of the day, she's been laughing.

And I've been resisting the urge to kiss her. *Talking
about my dead brother to his pregnant wife, and I've had to
stop myself from kissing her. What kind of sick bastard am I?*

I look away, but not before I catch a look from Dad again. Unreadable.

Lucy stretches and yawns. "Time for bed." I don't even realize that I've said it out loud until she looks at me funny. But she only nods and kisses Mom goodnight, hugging Dad. She just frowns slightly at me and heads up the stairs.

Mom quickly gets up, too, and kisses my head goodnight. It's like she was on orders to go upstairs as soon as Lucy did, that Dad wanted to talk to me alone the first chance he got.

"So…" I was right. I get up and sit on the sofa, waiting for whatever he's going to say. "We were surprised when you said Lucy was coming with you…"

"So was she."

He nods, "She looks good. Happier. Healthier." I know they've seen her weekly. She's shown me all the baby stuff Mom brings each time. The den is looking like a nursery already and nothing's been moved or changed. So I know he's seen that she's healthier already. I only nod, still waiting.

Dad clears his throat and sits forward a little, leaning on his knees and clasping his hands in front of himself. It's his earnest pose. This usually accompanied a long lecture; a serious infraction had occurred and he wanted to make the punishment as long and drawn out as possible. "Jake." He looks up at me, a stare I've never been able to completely match. "Your mom and I like that you're taking good care of Lucy. That you're helping her so much…to get back to…well, to being happier. It's important for her and for the baby." I nod again. I know not to interrupt him when he's in lecture mode. And I'm still waiting for the punchline.

"I can see that you really care for her. That you want what's best for her." *This* is *going to be long and painful*. I nod again to get him to the point faster hopefully. "Well…" He sighs, sitting back finally, hands flat on his knees, "Are you in love with her?"

I was not expecting him to be this blunt. I thought he'd try to warn me against complicating things, to be a good brother, to her and Max, not ask me about my feelings.

I stammer, "Of course I love her…"

"No. You know what I'm asking you, boy. Answer me."

I only nod. It's all I can do. I haven't even admitted this feeling to myself. *Saying it out loud to him…no, can't do it. I can't admit to betraying Max. Not to Dad. Not to myself.*

He only nods too and rubs his hands over his face, sighing loudly. Then he fixes me with his stare again. "Family is important, Jake. It's everything to me really. I loved Alex the moment I saw her in that coffee shop. I saw her sweetness buried under the hard life she had. I saw what she *could* become. Having you boys in my life…well, that's just been…more than I ever thought I'd get in this world."

He's never spoken to me like this, this warm. He's been encouraging, supporting, giving before. But not warm. Not really. It makes me a little uncomfortable. I don't know how to respond to him, so I only nod.

"Everyone deserves a chance at that kind of love. The kind you *can't* control; *it* controls you." I nod. "If that's what you have for Lucy…then you shouldn't let…you shouldn't let anything stand in the way of seeing if she could feel the same about you." I can only nod, feeling the tears in my eyes that I see in his too. "But if you're only acting on some sense of obligation to Max…to take care of his…" He shakes his head, unable to finish. He doesn't need to. *I know what he's saying.*

It's the same question I had. Briefly. But I know something he doesn't. I've been fighting this need for Lucy since the moment I met her. I never would've acted on it, not while she was with Max. But I've known I've loved her, even if I couldn't admit it to myself.

"I love her." I say it quietly, before laughing a little and sitting back too, running my hands through my hair. "I don't know what to do about it…but I do…"

He nods, but stays quiet. He finally gets up and pats me on the shoulder, only adding, "Just be sure of what you want to do before you do anything…for her sake."

I stay downstairs for a long time, walking out to the terrace and listening to the waves.

I cry quietly to myself. For Max. For Lucy. For myself. *This is all fucked up.*

When I admitted to her how I felt, that day she was stuck in my elevator, I never imagined that I'd get a chance to act on it. *I thought I was purging myself of the feelings by getting them out. Here, you take this crap, Lucy. It's yours, my heart. Now throw it away, so I can get on with my miserable life.*

I sniff and suck in the cool, wet air. I already pledged to Max that I would take care of her. No matter what. That I'd take care of his child. No matter what.

But what has me stopping my tears cold isn't thoughts of Max and what he'd think of me wanting to be with Lucy.

It's thoughts of what could happen if I *wasn't* with her. I know I won't want anyone else. I might be able to try to make something work, but I'd always know I missed my chance at happiness. Just like I said.

And if Lucy were ever to be with another man...I look down at my hands. They are two fists shaking against my knees. *This isn't anger. This is rage. A rage I've never felt before. I only tasted it a little that night that asshole had his hand on her. But she wasn't mine then.*

I don't know if it was the implied blessing from Mom and Dad. The admitting out loud to loving her. Or the realization that I would take care of Lucy how Max would've taken care of her. That he'd want me to protect her and keep her. But my indecision is gone.

She was never meant to be anyone else's except Max's...but fate stepped in. And I will *make her mine.*

58 Her

"Thanks again for this weekend, Jake. It was exactly what I needed…" I hug him again, still not going into my building though.

"I'm glad. I know it meant a lot to Mom and Dad. They miss seeing you more." Jake looks down at the big bag of baby stuff next to my other bag. He laughs. "Sure you don't need some help getting all this upstairs?"

"No. Thanks." I start to pick up both bags, but leave them on the sidewalk and stand to face him again. I tried to tell him this in the car on the drive back, but I didn't have the courage. I didn't want anything to upset the nice weekend.

"I…I don't know how you always know just what I need…to get me out of my head. To get me to a better place again, but I…I really want to say thank you." I swallow and look down. "The Fourth was supposed to be the anniversary…of Max telling me he loved me." I look back up at him and smile. It's not a tearless smile, but still a happy one. "I don't know how I would've gotten through it without you."

I throw my arms around him again and kiss his scruffy cheek. He presses against me a little more. But lets me go quickly.

Inside my apartment, alone again, I still feel the glow of a weekend spent with family. I talked with Mom and Dad a lot over the weekend too. I even talked with Cathy. She knew I was having a hard time lately. She and PJ invited me out to Downers Grove for the parade and fireworks too. But she sounded extra happy for me that I was spending the whole weekend away instead.

I move around the apartment, putting yet another bag of stuff into the den. It's starting to look cluttered and like a nursery exploded on top of an office. I'll have to think about getting rid of some furniture soon. This thought only sends a small shiver of fear and sadness through me. I've been reluctant to make any changes to the apartment so far. *I can face this. I know Jake will help me too, if I ask.*

Heading into the bedroom, I go back to thinking more about this weekend.

It wasn't just hearing stories about Max, him as a teenager, as a young man. It was being around all of them that made me feel better. I love my own family, but Max's family became such a big part of my life so quickly, that I didn't even realize how much I'd missed seeing them until this weekend.

Ron is so much like Max. Or well, Max was so much like him. Strong, silent type. He didn't say much to me all weekend, but he smiled a lot. And what he did say was sweet. Stern, but sweet. He acted like I would've expected Max to act. Silently making sure that I had everything I need, while admonishing me if he thought I wasn't doing something to take care of myself.

Alex though was a little different this visit. She was softer somehow. She kept her arms around me a lot more. We cried a lot together. And laughed. I felt closer to her than I ever have before. Like we understood each other more.

I know she had a hard life before Ron. I asked her about my baby's great-grandparents. She looked sad, but said she's never spoken to them, not since they kicked her out when they found out she was pregnant with Max as a teenager. It made me feel protective of her, like Max always said he felt.

Last night, though, *that* was a conversation I wasn't prepared for with her. She took me for a walk along the retaining wall, just us. And when she talked then, I could see a lot of Max in her, glimpses of a strength I hadn't really seen before.

She told me about a conversation she had with Max that I didn't know about. It was about a month before he passed. He said he knew I was struggling with him, that he wanted her advice on what he could do to help me. She said, "To help you be your best, your strongest. For him and for yourself and for any child he hoped you'd give him." Her eyes were shining with tears in the sunset, but her voice didn't shake, she didn't pause.

She went on to tell me that the advice she gave him was simple and even silly probably, nothing concrete. But she did tell him one thing. And she wanted to tell me the same thing.

She stopped our walk and faced me then. I was actually a little scared of what she was going to say. I don't know why, but I felt like the whole weekend had led up to that conversation.

She put her hands on my shoulders gently and said, "I told Max that when love comes into our lives, it's a gift. What we do with that gift is up to us. That for a woman, at least for a certain kind of woman, it takes a strong man to bring out the best in us. To help us to realize our potential for loving, for giving all of our unique gift of love in return."

I remember nodding at this point. It's how I felt with Max. That he was special. That I'd never know another man who was able to balance me, to be the dominant force I crave still. So I could give my greatest gift, my submission and heart.

I told her that I understood what she meant. That Max did take her advice. I remember a special night of love and tenderness with him. I pat my stomach and said it may have even been the night we conceived. She liked that thought.

I don't remember the rest of what she said, except at the end. She stopped us again before heading up the path to the house. She didn't look at me though this time. She looked at the porch, where Jake and Ron were waiting for us.

I remember this part word for word. "You have a lot of life ahead of you. Our family is strong. You can lean on our strength as much as you need. Or want. Just always keep your heart open, to accept the gifts that are given to you. Always."

I went to bed last night with her words in my head. They mirrored my own thoughts. That my heart will never heal from losing Max, but I've come to terms with reality.

Ya know what they say about reality and I can tell ya, that bitch bites hard! I laugh, patting my belly. *Sorry, Max, I'll try to keep from cursing around our child.*

But my reality is a hard one to face. I'm alone. Large with child. I giggle thinking about Laura's voice when she says this. *I don't want to be alone forever. But I don't know that I can open myself up to anyone. Ever again.*

It felt good to know though, that if I ever did, I would still have Max's family too. That's what she was trying to tell me. That no matter what my future holds, they'll all love me and be there for me and our child. I'll always have Max and his family. Always.

59 Him

Today. I'm going to say something to her today. I've waited long enough.

Well, not really. Max has only been gone for a little over three short months. But I've watched Lucy go through the full gamut of emotions. I've watched her pull herself together again. I've watched and waited.

I debated about talking to her on the drive home from the lake house. But she was so happy, relaxed. And I didn't want to be distracted with traffic. I want to sit down with her, over dinner. *To tell her the feelings I shared before...that they haven't gone away. That I want her. God, how I want her.*

I've been thinking all week about what I want to say to her, how I want to take this slow, to not pressure her. *I know it's going to be hard though...to not rush into this. I want to rush her right into my bed!*

Okay. Not helping. I have a long day ahead of me, running around to different project sites with project managers. *I do not need to have painful balls again.*

"Hey." Lucy lifts her head up from a report and smiles at me. She looks pretty today, soft. Thankfully, she's not wearing anything that shows her growing tits too much. "Let's get dinner tonight."

She smiles, "Can't. I have plans with Laura tonight."

I frown. I think about pushing her. I know I could. I smile again, "Okay. Tomorrow night then." She nods and goes back to her report as I turn away.

Probably best to give myself a little more time to think about what all I want to say anyway. I want to be clear with her. *I'm offering her my love, and definitely not the brotherly kind.* I smile on the way down to my car.

I smile for the rest of the day, even while yelling at a project manager for messing up later.

60 Her

"Ya know, you could get into trouble for that?"

I turn in the checkout line and see a tall man in a light brown suit standing very close to me. His blue eyes are crinkled with a small laugh and big smile. I laugh, with another carrot from the salad bar in my hand, halfway to my mouth already, "Oops. Busted."

"There's penalties for stealing, you know? …Hardened criminals like you should be dealt with harshly." Something in the way he says this makes me shiver. He's leaning a little too close, almost whispering into my ear. His deep voice is like a drum against the beat of my heart.

I hear myself saying, "A good spanking perhaps…" and have to hide my shocked look by turning around. *I can't believe I just said that out loud! To a total stranger*! I move a little away from him, but I can feel that he moves even closer, chuckling behind me. *Good, he took it as a joke anyway.*

Before I can stop him, he tells the cashier that he's paying for both our lunches. "Oh...thanks...but I got it." I pull the money out of my pocket I had ready.

He pushes my hand down and hands his money to the woman instead. She just shrugs and gives him his change.

I walk a little away and turn around to put my tray in between us. He's standing close still. "Thank you."

"I only did it so you'd have to sit with me." He smiles more. He has nice eyes when he smiles. "You can confess how you got started on your life of crime. And we can discuss an appropriate punishment for salad bar infringement."

I only smile and sit down at the first table I see. He sits across from me and keeps smiling. "Your name's Lucy, right?" I'm startled and stop smiling. "Sorry! I didn't mean to scare you. I'm not some stalker or anything. I come here almost every day. I've seen you here a lot too. And I've heard your co-workers call you by name."

"Oh...yeah. This is close to my office. You work around here too?"

"Yeah, around the block. Sad to say, there are days when this is breakfast, lunch and dinner for me." He puts out his hand, "I'm Jason. I'm glad to finally officially meet you, Lucy."

I shake his hand. I feel a little tingle in my stomach. This is the first man I've touched in a long time, a stranger anyway. The tingle is a mix of excitement and guilt. But I ignore the guilt for now.

We spend the lunch hour laughing and comparing places to eat in the neighborhood. He's an account manager for a large real estate investment firm. For some reason, when I talk about my job, I don't mention that I'm just helping out my brother-in-law. *For some reason?*

Be honest in your own head, girl. You're flirting with this hottie. And somehow mentioning that you're not really working, you're just filling in until you pop out your baby might put a damper on the obvious flirting he's doing too.

I look at my watch. A constant reminder of Max. I feel the twinge of guilt again. But I push it back once more. "I better get going. My boss is strict about being on time." *An understatement.* Traeger men cannot stand any breach of punctuality. And there's an office meeting this afternoon.

"Oh. Well…" Jason smiles and stands. "I'd like to see you again. How bout dinner this weekend?"

And for some reason I say yes. I even give him my phone number. I walk away a little dazed. I knew he was flirting, but I didn't think he'd ask me out.

I am so out of practice in this whole dating thing.

Not that it matters. I might go to dinner with him. Once. But it's not going to go anywhere. It can't, right? I mean. Gee, Jason, I'd really like to hang out more with you, but you see, my water just broke and I have to get to the hospital. Sexy.

I'm laughing at myself when I get to the office.

No harm in practicing a little flirting though, right? I don't have to tell this guy anything. I can just go out once, split the check, have some fun and be done with it.

But I keep thinking about Jason's hands and smile during the office meeting. I keep thinking about how he had just a little bit of a dominant attitude... *Maybe... or maybe it's just wishful thinking, girl.*

I'm so completely distracted; I don't notice when Jake asks me something about an order for a client. I answer him quickly, but shrink when he gives me a narrow look a little later. *I know that look. The Look.*

I hurry out of the conference room when the meeting ends to avoid having to talk to him.

61 Him

I say goodbye to staff walking by my office on their way out. I glance at my computer screen. Lucy will be leaving for the day soon. Most everyone's gone already. I like to offer summer hours to anyone who wants them. Come in early, leave early, as long as it doesn't interfere with production or project progress. It's worked out so far.

I pick up my phone and dial her extension. "Come to my office." I don't wait for her reply; I hang up. I don't have to wait long for her to arrive. She must've already been ready to leave, because she has her bag with her.

"Shut the door, girl." I like how her face flushes at my angry tone. She had this same flush in the meeting a few hours ago. She quietly closes the door and sits down in the chair opposite my desk. I get up and move around to sit on the edge of the desk, my arms crossed in front of me. She tries to avoid looking up. "Wanna tell me why I had to ask you a question twice this afternoon?"

She only shakes her head. "No, you don't want to tell me?" I can see I'm making her uncomfortable. Her fingers keep moving against each other on her lap. "Look at me when I'm talking to you, girl." She lifts her bright blue eyes to meet mine.

"I'm sorry. I…I wasn't listening in the meeting." She swallows.

And suddenly her look of nervousness makes me nervous. I drop my arms and anger, standing up straight, "Are you okay? Feeling okay?" She looks a little paler.

She laughs even more nervously, "Yes. I'm fine. Really…just wasn't paying attention is all. I won't let it happen again, boss." She sits up and tries for a light smile.

"So what had you so distracted then?" I'm heading back to anger pretty quickly, to hide how scared I felt at the thought of anything being wrong.

Her look is strange. *Nervous and shy*? Like she wants to bolt from here. "I…I'd rather not say." She crinkles her nose. This is a look I've seen on her before. Her "tell" that she's withholding something. She's only done this a few times with me. Usually teasing whatever it is out of her is pretty easy though.

I'm not in the mood to tease now. "You better start talking, girl."

"Fine. If you must know. I have a date."

I blink and sit back on the edge of the desk. I feel like I've been punched in the gut.

62 Her

"You have a date? Tonight?"

"No. This weekend. Maybe. I don't know. This guy I met at lunch asked me out on a date." I laugh. It feels strange saying this to Jake. He certainly looks strange hearing it, all frown and disbelief. I'm nervously babbling. "It was so out of the blue and completely ridiculous, that I said yes. I was laughing at myself and distracted, so I'm…"

"You're not going." His face is stone, voice flat and deep.

"What?"

"You heard me. You're not going." He hasn't moved, his face hardly even moved in speaking, his jaw set so strong.

Now it's my turn to frown in disbelief and a little anger. "That's not up to you, Jake."

He laughs, still not changing his stony glare though. "Yeah. It is. And you're not going out with *some* guy you just met. You're not going out with anyone, Lucy."

I laugh. "It's really not your call, Jake. I'm a big girl. I can decide for myself. And he's nice. I don't think you have to worry so much about me."

"Worry about you?" He shakes his head and grins at me. "You are a stupid girl sometimes, Lucy."

"You're stupid if you think I'm going to sit here and take being insulted by you, Jake!" I stand and am immediately shoved straight back down, hard, into the seat by his right hand. But he hardly moved. His hand is already back crossed over his chest. He looks almost relaxed, leaning against his desk.

"I meant to have this talk with you over a nice dinner tomorrow. But I don't see any reason to wait now." He rubs his chin a little. I frown, waiting for his explanation of why he's acting so strange. His glare pierces me again and I sit back more, crossing my legs.

63 Him

Everything I had prepared to say is out of my head now. Replaced by this rage. That another man asked Lucy out. And she accepted.

I had intended to be gentle, to ease her into a discussion of the night she came to my building. To remind her of our deep friendship and how much I care about her. There's no chance at gentleness now.

"You remember when I told you how much you mean to me?" She only blinks. Thrown off by my blunt anger that doesn't match my words. "That night you were stuck in my elevator?"

She swallows and nods slowly. "You're not ever going out with anyone else, Lucy." I watch as her face flushes again and she looks like she's going to say something. "Interrupt me now, girl, and you'll be sitting on a red ass for the rest of what I have to say." Her lips press tightly closed again.

"I'm through waiting. I don't really know if you're ready. I don't care. I'm done waiting for you to be ready for me." I grab her arms and yank her off the chair, pulling her against me. I kiss her.

Not the soft kiss I gave her that night. There's nothing sweet about this kiss. But she responds. Her tongue pushes against mine, her lips soften. And her tiny moan escapes before I pull my face back to look into her eyes again. She takes her time opening them slowly.

"*That's* why you're not going out with anyone else, Lucy."

64 Her

His grin is the first thing I see when I reopen my eyes. I can't think of anything to say besides, "Oh." Jake lets go of my arms, but I stay standing close, in between his legs. I can see that he's turned on. *I know I am.*

I've thought of Jake this way before, just never really thought it would happen. I had started to put him in the friend file in my mind. That was not a friendly kiss though. I brush my lips with two fingers.

He's still grinning, watching my hand and mouth, searching my eyes. "I've waited a long time to do that."

I move a step back from him. I'm rocked by a clear image of Max. How *he* was so angry that night; how *he* was so loving the next day. How he's gone. *But I still shouldn't be here, doing this now. And certainly not with his brother.* "You shouldn't have done that…it's too soon for me…for this."

His grin falters for a moment, his voice takes on a little of the anger he had earlier, "But it's not too soon for you to go out with some random guy you just met?"

I push against his chest, but his arms lock around me again, "That's not fair, Jake. That was just going to be one night. One time. Not this. Not you."

"Why *not* me, Lucy? You've known how I feel about you. You've *had* to know. What? Did you think I'd wait, sit back and watch you get over Max by being with other men first?"

"I don't want to get over Max!"

"Too bad!" And he kisses me again. Just as hard, just as forceful. This time I push away from him. Or try to anyway. His arms are stones around me, keeping me from moving. I can feel my body reacting to him, wanting him. The same way I did that night. But my mind is still running away. Or trying to.

Jake finally stops and lets me move a little in his arms. I pull my hand up and slap him hard, stinging my own hand and seeing the redness on his cheek.

65 Him

Her little slap stings for a second. She holds her hand though like it hurt her more. I let go of her and gently pull her hands apart, keeping my eyes locked on hers. I kiss her palm and press it against my cheek.

"You can kick and scream and fight me all you want, Lucy. But I'm through waiting to have what I want." I grin again. "I want you."

She tries to bolt again, pulling her hand away and moving back. I grab her and twist us around, pushing her on to the desk. I'm gentle though. I put my knee in between her legs, keeping myself off of her stomach, pressing only her upper body into the desk, holding her hands down.

"I *want* you, Lucy. I *know* you want me. I can feel it. I can see it. I can taste it." I kiss her again. She's still resisting a little, but she moans too. "And I *will* have you. You *will* belong to me."

"No. Stop. This is all wrong." Her tears choke her words and she tries to push against my hands. I just grin, not moving. I bend down and kiss her neck; she tilts her head back against the wood for a moment, exposing more for me. But just as quickly, she shakes her head and pushes against my hands again.

"This isn't wrong, Lucy. We're right together." I growl my words softly, biting her ear to keep her head from moving, brushing her neck with my stubbled chin. Her nipples answer nicely.

"You shouldn't be doing this, Jake. Please…" But there's not much strength in her words, her breathing is too fast.

I kiss her again and she responds a little better, opening her lips quickly. But the next second, she's still trying to push against me. "I should've done this a long time ago."

That apparently was the wrong thing to say. She increases her pushing, her eyes flashing with anger. "No. This *is* wrong. I can't do this to Max. Get off me, Jake!" She's trying with all her might to push me, I let up just a little so she doesn't hurt herself.

"Max isn't here, Lucy. *I* am. And I won't take no for an answer." I run my tongue up the side of her neck and grab her ear between my teeth again, not letting go as I whisper, "Not when I can feel you saying yes." I kiss her cheek gently.

But she twists her head around, glaring at me. "What? Are you going to rape me, Jake? Rape your brother's wife?"

"I will if I have to…" I grin at her shocked reaction, "but I don't think I'll have to."

She bucks and squirms against my grip, but she's no match, hardly moving me. Actually only getting me harder. When she stops finally, "And you're no one's wife…Max is dead, girl, it's time you get that through your head."

She screams. A primal, outraged, from the gut scream and this time when she bucks, she moves me. She moves the desk. I slam her arms down harder on it to get her to stop. She digs her nails into my hands. I don't let go, I just let her scream until she wears herself out. It doesn't take long. She dissolves into tears for a longer stretch. Tossing her head side to side, hiding under curls, her whole body rocking against me. I wait this out too.

I want to kiss her, to stop her tears with gentleness. *But I know that's not what she needs. And it's not all I want to do.*

"That's enough, girl. Stop crying." I laugh at her little sniffle in response to my command, how she manages to make it sound defiant and angry. But she stops. She doesn't look at me though. She looks at my mouth. Watches my lips as I talk to her.

"Your life didn't end just because Max's did. I know how he felt about you. That you belonged to him. I know you think that the only way to keep him in your heart is to close it off to me. That he'd want it that way." She raises her eyes briefly to mine. *I've got her number.*

I laugh at her and she lowers her eyes again. "He wanted you to be happy, Lucy. If *he* couldn't make you happy for the rest of your life, I know..." *Dammit*. I take a deep breath. "I *know* he'd never forgive me if I didn't try."

She looks at me again, tears stuck in place, magnifying the red and blue. *I want to taste her tears. I want to cause her tears not from this emotional pain, but from my hands. I want to take her by force.*

But I only take her mouth again. I slam my lips against hers, shoving her head hard against the wood, crushing and clutching her fingers in mine. Her little cry and gasp are lost to my breaths. I don't wait for her lips to open to me, I pry them open with my tongue. I explore every part of her mouth, biting her lips, biting her tongue, choking her with mine. I pull away and lower my forehead onto her chest. *I want to take all of her this way.*

But I know that I'll enjoy it more, taking her one piece at a time. I lift my head up and put my finger over her swollen lips. Pressing them hard against her teeth. She's panting. "Your lips are mine now." She nods, blinking the tears down into her hair. "Say it." I cup her cheek and feel the cold path of her tears against her hot skin.

"My lips are yours…" Almost no sound, just her beautiful mouth forming the words I've longed to hear.

"Good." I let her go and walk around to the other side of my desk again. I watch her slowly get up and move her skirt down, run her hands through her hair.

She doesn't look at me again, only reaches for her bag and moves slowly towards the door. I wait till she has it open before saying anything more. "Lucy." She turns, but still doesn't look up all the way. "Cancel that date. Tell him you're taken."

She whispers, but I can just hear, "Yes, Sir."

66 Her

I'm shaky walking to the elevator. *Luckily no one is around. No one heard me screaming. No one heard Jake.*

I lean against the wall of the elevator, holding my mouth. I can still feel where he bit my lip. My tongue keeps seeking out the spot, wanting more of him.

Jeff gives me a concerned frown. I must look a mess. "You okay?" I nod and his hand is gentle as he opens the door and helps me inside.

I want to cry or laugh or both. I'm wrecked. Fragmented. Mental looney right now.

I try to hold onto what Jake said, not how he made me feel. I can't help crossing my legs in frustration though.

I said yes to a date, not because I thought I was ready for one. I've been horny as hell, but I know nothing would've happened with a stranger. I didn't even want anything to happen. It was just a step. That was all. A step into the world of the living. That was all I thought I was ready for.

Jake isn't a stranger though. He's family.

Okay, I've wanted him…like I wanted Max. I've responded to him like I responded to Max. I put my hands over my face, hiding my emotions from Jeff again. From myself.

I can't face this. All this. The feelings of guilt, desire, anger…love.

I take a deep breath and look out the window to continue hiding most of my face. So I can face the truths. *I want Jake. I want him to want me. To possess and dominate me. To order me around. To do whatever he pleases just like he just did.*

But he's not Max. I don't know that I can be like that with anyone again. I can't face giving all of myself to someone again. Not even Jake.

67 Him

I haven't been in the office all day. Probably a good thing. I've had a hard enough time concentrating on anything besides our dinner tonight.

I've worked from home, on my home and other projects. Mitch has been running back and forth. I've kept tabs on Lucy this way pretty easily. I half expected her not to come in today. I thought she might try to avoid me after yesterday. I'm glad that she didn't.

I smile to myself. *I wouldn't have let her, but I'm glad that I won't have to resort to that.*

I hear the buzzer from downstairs and glance at the clock in my kitchen. *Good girl, right on time.* I hit the intercom, "Come on up. Elevator's working now."

I open the front door. But I don't hear the elevator running. My buzzer sounds again. I roll my eyes. "Yes?"

"I'm not coming in. I know you told Jeff to bring me here, but I've already texted him to come right back. I'm going home."

"He won't be coming back, Lucy. I told him that I'll be getting you home tonight." I wait for her to swallow that news. *It's a lie.* "Now. Get your ass inside and up here." I buzz her in again, holding down the button longer this time. I'm already texting Jeff not to return. He replies back with a smile only. I roll my eyes again.

I can hear the elevator running this time.

I stand at the door waiting for her. When the doors open, I'm a little surprised. She looks great. But different.

It's her outfit. Lucy's wear a dark blue silky V-neck top that shows off a lot more cleavage than I've seen from her before, but it isn't too much. And dark jeans. I smile watching her legs move, her toes peeking out of high-heeled sandals.

She stops in front of me, but she's not smiling. "I only came up to wait for a cab."

I hesitate for a moment. Deciding. I'd planned to start over, to try for the gentleness I was originally planning. But seeing her like this, with her hair full and bouncy, chin and eyes all set defiant and on edge, and in clothes obviously meant to piss me off. I can't help myself. *The road of best intentions, right?*

I grab her arms quickly and pick her up; she squeals. I turn quickly and put her down inside and against the wall with a little shove. Her eyes are wide with shock, but she's recovering fast. I stop anymore nonsense she might try by closing the door and standing in front of it. "You're not leaving until you've had dinner. So you might as well make yourself comfortable."

Lucy narrows her eyes, but finally moves more into the loft. "And if you did call a cab, you better cancel it right now. Because if I have to go downstairs to get rid of one, your ass will be very sore when I get back up here, girl."

She reluctantly pulls out her phone and texts something. "Good. Now come sit down. We have a few things to discuss before eating."

I watch her walk over to my sofa. *Her ass looks great.* "I've never seen you in jeans before."

She turns with a wicked smile, "That's because *Max*, your *brother*, wouldn't let me wear pants. Does it bother you?"

So that's her game. She thinks mentioning Max, his rules will throw me off, that I'll back down and give up trying, that I'll think about him more than her. Sorry, brother, but she's here. You're not. And I want her for myself now.

I grin, I believe Max would've wanted it this way. *He didn't really want anyone to have Lucy of course. But he knew her. Loved her. He would know she needs to give her love and to be loved in return. She's only happiest when she can really give herself freely. And she'll only give herself to me. I'm very sure of that.*

"I think you look sexy." Her little wicked smile falters, I only grin more. "Maybe a little too sexy for the office. But I like it."

She sits down, with a little pouty frown that she quickly tries to hide. "So you don't think girls should only wear skirts or dresses, just like *Max* and Ron?"

I'll give her an A for effort. "Nope. I told you before that I thought Max had too many rules and didn't let you make enough decisions for yourself." I sit next to her, handing her a glass of milk. She frowns at this too, but takes it. "I'll of course tell you if I don't like something that you wear. Or if I don't think it's appropriate. And in those cases, you will, of course, change." I like how red her face gets. *So easy to push her buttons.*

"You just said you like a girl to make her own decisions." She's trying for bratty, but I can hear the real question in her voice.

"Lucy, this is what I want to talk to you about." I cut the crap. As fun as it is to see her squirm like this, I know we have to have a serious talk about everything, to clear the air about what *I* want and what she needs.

68 Her

I made Laura go shopping with me instead of dinner yesterday. I made her help me pick out these jeans and top. She was surprised that I wasn't getting more maternity clothes and that I was looking for tight and revealing instead. This was never really my taste. But I didn't tell her why.

And this isn't overly tight or revealing. My belly wouldn't fit in anything too tight right now. I look down at the amount of cleavage popping out of this shirt though and want to cover up. I had a sweater on in the office all day, but I'm not going to tell Jake that.

I planned to flaunt my independence in his face. *To show him that I'm not his puppy, not Max's puppy anymore either.* I knew my plan was in trouble the moment I saw the look on his face at the door. I could see how turned on he was by how I looked.

It wasn't the reaction I was expecting. *I know he's not exactly like Max. I haven't been able to put my finger on what's different though. That I've had more freedom around him maybe? And more indecision. I don't know exactly what Jake wants or thinks. It's frustrating.*

"I want to be clear with you, Lucy. I don't want there to be any doubt in your mind." I only nod. He looks soft, but determined. He takes my hand in both of his. I like how warm and strong his hands are. There's little calluses on his palms, from working to fix this place up. "I'm not Max. I won't ever be Max."

I try to pull my hand away, but he keeps it locked in his, "I know that!" I'm getting upset again. *I know I was the one to bring Max up, but I really don't want to talk about him, not like this.* Holding hands with Jake.

"Don't interrupt me again, girl. I'll let you know when it's your turn to speak." *See right there. Different. Max probably would've slapped me or turned me over his knee for talking back.* I only nod. I'm pulled between this urge to push him, to see how far I *could* push him and this need to see how different he really is.

He takes a deep breath and starts again. "I'm not going to dictate every part of your life, every minute by minute." He puts his hand on my cheek and rubs down my neck, following down my arm to our hands again. "I don't think that's what you need to be my good girl, Lucy." I shiver from his touch and his words. "I'll have plenty of rules, sure. And lots of consequences. But I'll expect you to make a lot of decisions on your own. And if I disapprove of any, I'll give you fair warning."

"You're talking…" I realize I'd interrupted him, so I stop. *Puppy*!

But he nods and smiles, "Go on."

"Jake…you're talking like we're already together…like everything's already decided…"

He grins again, "It is. I told you last night. You belong to me."

I open my mouth a few times to answer, but I'm not sure what to say. He laughs and I get angry again at this. "Stop laughing at me! I don't like it when you do that."

He only laughs harder for a moment, before trying to swallow back more chuckling, he finally ends with a big crooked smile again. "I'm sorry. I don't mean to laugh at you. But you're just so damn cute when you try to be something you're not." He pulls me forward and kisses me, but just a light kiss. "You're not in charge, Lucy. You never will be. So don't try to act all independent and strong-willed with me anymore. I'll bend you over for a good spanking if you try it again tonight."

"I'm not *trying* for anything…except to make you understand how I feel!"

"So tell me then." But he gives me a stern look, "But lower your voice or you'll be sitting on a stool in the corner and getting a good time out along with that spanking."

I blink at this image. *Max always just got angry, ballistic angry sometimes. He'd make me recite rules facing the wall. But the image of being treated like such a child by Jake…I'm shaken by this.*

He didn't say it with anger either. I'm not even sure he is angry right now. I don't know how to respond to this. To him. I don't know what he really wants from me.

"You're confusing me…I don't know what you want. I always knew exactly what…" I can't finish. I can't bring Max up again.

He shakes his head. "I know what I want with you, Lucy. And I want to be clear about it. No confusion." He stops though and lets go of my hand. He takes a big drink of his beer before turning back to me. "I know what you had with Max. I don't want that. Not *exactly* that. Shit. This is harder to put into words, to explain…" He takes a deep breath while looking up at his ceiling.

"I'll give you an example. Maybe that's the easiest way to explain it." He stares at me again and I only nod. "If I tell you the sky is beige. I'd expect you to argue with me, right?" I nod, laughing a little at his choice of example. "But you wouldn't have argued with Max if he said it, would you?" His voice takes on a deep edge, full of emotion.

I shake my head. *As ridiculous as his example is, I know it's true. I wouldn't have argued with anything Max ever said or did. No matter how minor or major. I knew I'd be punished.*

"I expect you to respect me. To obey me." His voice is so low it's almost a whispered growl. "I won't accept *any* disrespect or back talk from you. But I *will* allow you to speak your mind with me." He grins, "Not in public…but privately, with me…we can discuss anything."

I nod. Again, a little startled and shaken by the differences. *And similarities*. I frown with a pouty smile, "So I can't argue with you about the sky being beige around other people?" I'm being sarcastic, pushing him just a little.

He grins, "Sure you can. I'll know that you're asking me to give you a spanking with other people watching if you do." He laughs at my shocked reaction. "Give it a try, girl, if you think I won't do it."

I just lower my eyes at this image. He's relaxed and laughing, but I can hear the edge in his voice too. *He* would *punish me in front of other people.* The thought makes my head spin. And my pussy wet.

He lifts my chin to look in his eyes again. "And if I tell you to change your clothes, I'll expect no arguments. If I tell you a decision is final, then no arguments. If it's a rule, no arguments. But I don't want you to be so scared of me that you don't ever discuss anything with me. I won't be ruled by my anger, Lucy, and neither will you. Do you understand now how I want it to be with us?"

I nod, tears in my eyes. "I think so…"

He smiles again and pulls me forward for a deeper kiss. I melt against him, pulling with my lips, searching for more of him with my tongue. "You want to be my good girl, don't you?"

I nod again, tears falling freely down my face now, "Yes, Jake."

69 Him

It's all I was waiting for. I scoop her up under her legs and arms. Lucy doesn't say anything, just wraps her hands around my neck as I carry her into my bedroom.

I set her down next to the bed and she looks around, uncertain. *I know what she's thinking*. And for a moment I feel a startling amount of rage.

Jealousy again. My button she can push so easily. I know she's hesitating because of her thoughts of Max. And I have to take a deep breath to not react.

Instead I demand her full attention again with a stern voice, a little of the anger showing, "Lucy." Her blue eyes pop to mine and she stops biting her lower lip. I smile, satisfied that she's properly focused again.

I put my hands on her hips and pull them to me, pressing her against my chest for a kiss. She starts to lift her hands to my neck, but I stop her, "Keep your hands at your sides." I like her this way, open to me.

I explore her while kissing. My hands travelling over the silk top, across her stomach, up her arms, around her neck. I give a little squeeze with both hands, not hard, but her eyes open a little. I grin against her lips, but keep kissing.

I'll like being able to choke her more when she's not pregnant...when I can see her eyes begging me to stop while I let her have enough air to keep moaning for me. I grin again with that image. That I'll be able to do whatever I like to her. *Not yet, but soon.*

I lift the bottom of her top up and start to pull it off her, but she moves her hands quickly over her tits. She only breathes my name, "Jake?" scared and uncertain again. I let go of the shirt and step back.

"Take off your clothes, Lucy." I had planned to be gentle about it, to slowly undress her. But she's pissed me off now. Now, I'll humiliate her.

She still stands with her hands over her tits. I know what she responds to. *I know what she even expects maybe.* I grin, "Do you *want* me to slap you, girl? Is that what it's going to take?"

She shakes her head, tears in her eyes, lowering her head to hide under her hair. "I can't do this...I'm sorry..."

I move the step towards her again and like that she flinches a little. *At least she's not just scared of her own thoughts, she's scared of me too. She should be.* I grab her chin and pull her head up hard. "I'm not asking." I drop my hand and like that she keeps her head up still. She's shaking though and questioning with her eyes. *I know my girl. I know what she needs. And it's not what* she *thinks she needs.*

I run my finger down her nose and smile, my voice calm, almost gentle, "You're going to give all of yourself to me, Lucy." I continue running just my finger across her skin, down her neck, across her collarbone, her shoulder, her back as I tell her what I'm going to do to her. "I'm going to make every inch of you hurt tonight, leave every inch of you covered with the feel of my touch on you." She's breathing faster, swallowing and leaning towards me slightly. *My little pain slut.*

I lean in more too, to whisper next to her ear, my stubble rubbing hard against her delicate skin, "You can resist if you want to add to my fun, but I'm going to claim every inch of you tonight whether you like it or not." She lets out a tiny moan.

I know she's used to responding to anger, to submitting to it. But I don't need her to relieve my anger. I need her to relieve my desires. I'll train her to respond to my needs only. To enjoy the pain I want to inflict. The humiliation I want her to endure. My desire doesn't stop at punishing her…that's only the beginning.

I step back. Very gently, very slowly, with the deep edge she shakes to obey, "Take off your clothes, girl." She doesn't hesitate. But she is slow, a small smile on her lips that disappears under her shirt. I watch as she removes the rest.

I take another step back to admire her. She moves to cover herself with her hair and hands clasped in front. I shake my head. "Pull your hair back and keep your hands to your sides." She does. "Chin up, eyes up." I smile at her eager responsiveness. "I want your eyes on me at all times, girl. No looking down or hiding." She nods slightly.

"Open your legs a little. Good girl." I can see that she's starting to feel uncomfortable, exposed. I can almost ignore how hard my cock is. *I've waited for this. I could prolong this moment all night.*

She's as beautiful as I imagined, with her shoulders back, skin smooth and pale, nipples hard and deep pink. The small mound of hair hides how wet I know she is. Her ribs pop with her fast breathing. Her mouth opens just a little in anticipation of my touch. Her belly only has a small bump; a reminder that I'll need to be gentle with at least some parts of her tonight. *Not a problem...just too bad for the rest of her then.*

I grin wickedly at her and she shrinks, lowering her chin and raising her shoulders a little under my stare. But she quickly comes to attention again when I raise an eyebrow.

I move around her slowly, letting her feel only my breath on her skin. Letting her know that I'm staring at every inch of her. Not speaking though. I want to see how long she can last before breaking down. *Not long apparently.* "Jake?" I only just moved from standing behind her to her other side. She turned her head to keep me in her sights.

I put only one finger on her lips. "Shhh...I'm admiring my girl. Just stay still and silent." I lean in and brush my lips against her cheek. "Don't speak again before I give you permission."

I start over. Walking around her slowly again, still not touching. I take even more time standing behind her, admiring the beautiful curve of her back, her shoulder blades tensing like a tiny bird ready for flight. Her curls move with each breath and the small shaking of her body. Her neck strains to see me, but she stays in place.

Her bottom is perfection, two pale moons glowing, just waiting to turn red for me. She's arching her back, wanting to display herself, even if she is nervous. I can see the dimples just above her cheeks and want to kiss them. *Later.* Her legs twitch and her toes dance against the floor, but she stays in place.

I slowly move around to her other side again, watching as her breathing catches more. She's anticipating an end to her misery. *Poor girl...I'm only just getting started.* I watch the slope and fullness of her tits expand with each breath, her stomach tightening and toes dancing even more. Her fingers are clenched into fists.

"Relax your hands, beautiful." She slowly uncurls her fingers, shaking her wrists a little before stopping all movement again. Even her toes stop. "That's my good girl. This is how I want you. Completely open to me. Now take a deep breath in and hold it." She does, watching me. I smile. Her tits push out more. "Keep holding it." I watch as her eyes get a little teary, not blinking as she looks at me. I smile again. "Don't let go."

I slap her ass hard, across both cheeks in the middle. She gasps out in surprise, stepping forward with one foot at the impact. I growl, "Get back in position." She quickly responds. Trying to relax her whole body at once. I give her a moment to get her breathing under control.

"Again, breathe in, beautiful. And *don't* let go this time."
I wait a little longer, seeing her eyes plead. I don't let her see
my hand raise behind her though, so she's just as surprised by
the sting and sound. She keeps her breath from escaping, but
steps out of place still. She recovers quickly though to stand
with her legs open more. "Breathe out." She gasps and
breathes quickly for a moment. Her cheeks flushing nicely.

"Again. In." Her face twitches with a pleading question,
but she obeys, taking in a bigger breath. I move around to
stand behind her. She strains her neck to follow me. I slap her
left cheek with the back of my right hand, hard. She stays put
this time, but she whimpers a little. "Out." I hear her gasp.
"Good girl."

I walk around to the front of her. "Take my belt off and
hand it to me." Her cry is tiny, barely audible but I still give
her a stern look for it. She'll learn to obey direct orders
silently. She moves her fingers to delicately unfasten the
buckle. She pushes and pulls it gently off, taking her time. I
smile. *I don't mind. I'm going to take my time using it too.*

"Arms out to your sides." This obviously startles her.
She's already feeling exposed. She opens her mouth and
almost says something. I grin and raise an eyebrow. "You
think you have something you need to add? Too bad, my
sweet girl. Just stay silent." I tweak her nose with my finger
and laugh at her pout. I trace the finger down her body,
between her tits, feeling her stomach clench at the tickle and
press just the one finger against her wet clit. Her moan is loud.
But she keeps her arms up. I don't move the finger. I don't
need to, she's doing plenty of moving on her own, her hips
uncontrollably pulsing. I smile and pull my finger away, her
moan is loud again. "No crying. Stay *still* and stay *silent*." She

pouts more, but she relaxes back into the same position, watching me.

I move back so she can see my hands. I hold the small buckle in my right palm, wrapping most of the belt around my hand until only six inches of the belt hangs loose. It's a thin leather; I chose to wear it specifically to use tonight.

Her look of curiosity is almost enough to make me laugh. I only smile and walk around her. "Keep your face forward." She instantly turns her head back around. "And keep your arms up. If you lower them, I will start from the beginning, beautiful." I know her arms will be tired by the time I'm through.

I start with her right shoulder and shoulder blade. Letting the small strap lick her pale skin to a pretty pink. Her shocked cry is strangled with a quick swallow. I hit her again in the same spot. This time her cry is more of a soft hiss. "Good girl."

I bring the strap down on her left shoulder and she shudders, but keeps her cry in. I told her I wanted every inch of her to feel my touch, to hurt with my touch. I meant it. I like the small pink strap mark that forms. It will fade all too quickly. *But that'll only be incentive to do this again to her soon.*

I alternate the strap from arm to arm, working slowly, bringing it down to wrap around her thin arms every few inches. When I get to her wrists, I stop. I let her breathe for a moment, watching as her lined arms shake with the effort of keeping them up, with the effort of staying silent. I step closer to her, feeling her heat against my shirt. I put my left hand in her hair and rub her head, saying softly into her left ear,

"Lower your arms and cross them in front of you." I can feel her shudder of relief. I grab her hair and twist it a little, yanking slightly on her head, before dropping it around to her front.

I step back and bring the strap down a little harder across her upper back. She tries for a hiss, but a small cry escapes too quickly. I hit her again in the same spot and her body shakes, but she manages to stay quiet this time. "Good girl." I follow the same slow pattern down her back, alternating side to side. I can hit her a little harder here, keep the marks a little longer. When these fade, I'll bring her back to stand in this position again. I'll like seeing her cover these in the office, making her expose the tiny bruises to me, kissing each before falling asleep each night.

When I get to her lower back, the sweet dip before the swell of her hips, I stop. I allow her time to breathe a little more. "Take a deep breath in and hold it." She does and I bring the strap down on her right side, following quickly with a second sting to her hip on the right too. I gave her the lightest touch of the strap, but this is a sensitive spot. She releases her breath with a series of hiccupped gulps. I allow it this time. It will be a long time before I can hit her midsection the way I want to. But I'm patient. The small bending and shaking is more than I'll allow though. "Stand up straight or tell me you want me to start over, girl!" She's instantly back in position. I pet her head again, "That's my sweet, good girl."

I know she'll tense more for the left side now, in anticipation of the pain. "Relax, beautiful." I watch her try to. "Deep breath for me, that's a good girl." I don't wait, I bring the strap down twice quickly on the left side and she lets her breath out with the same stuttered hiccupping and shaking moves. But she recovers a little faster, standing up a little quicker on her own.

I move around to her front. Her arms are still pink, only a few of the marks already fading. "Put your hands out together, palms up." She blinks her tears down her cheeks. And I have to stop. I grab her neck with my left hand and pull her towards me, kissing the trail of her tears on both cheeks, tasting her sweet saltiness. My mouth covers hers and I pull and bite at her lips. She's breathless again when I let her go, her hands clutching the front of my shirt.

I move back a little. "Palms up." She moves with a clear shake in her hands. I smile. Her look of fear is gorgeous, eyes wet and wide, but soft. I know if I put my hand between her legs again, I'll feel how needy she is. "You are my little pain slut, aren't you?" She freezes, blushes and looks down quickly. "Eyes up, girl!"

She pops her eyes to me again, but I can see her shame. I put my hand around her neck again and kiss her gently, whispering, "You are beautiful this way," against her cheek. I step back and she steadies her hands in front of her chest. I grin a little and keep my eyes on hers. I bring the belt up so she can see the small strap, waiting, giving her time to anticipate this strike.

I bring it down hard across her palms and watch her face squeeze closed. She held her breath on her own this time, releasing it with a slow whining hiss. She starts to close her hands, "No." She slowly opens them again with her eyes and I kiss each palm gently. "Hands behind your back, but keep your palms out." I won't let her squeeze the pain away.

I push her hair back again, exposing both her hard nipples and swelling tits. I know her tits may be like her middle, an area I can't touch like I want to…yet. To test her sensitivity, I squeeze her left nipple with my fingers, gentle at first, only adding a little pressure. She's gasping and panting with only a slight increase. I grin, bending my head down and licking her sore nipple. She starts to moan, but remembers herself and swallows this away, panting again. I move to her right nipple, flicking it between my tongue and teeth. She tries to cover her moan with a soft catch in her throat.

"Your tits are too sensitive, girl. I'll have to spank your ass twice as long to make up for not being able to give them my full attention tonight." She actually blushes more somehow. Her cheeks flaming red like her back and arms. She squirms a little, but stays put.

I step back and to the side. "On the bed," I grin as she shrinks back a little, "on all fours, girl." She starts to shake her head, but I grab her by the hair and stop her from moving at all. "Are you shaking your head no to me?" She blinks in fear, I shake her head, "Answer me."

"No…No, Sir."

I yank her hair harder, watching her eyes close against the pain. I walk her over to the bed this way, not letting go. To her credit, she keeps her hands behind her back. But this only makes me think about her obeying another before me. *I don't care that it was Max. I still don't like the thought being in her head now.*

"Put your hands to your sides." She does quickly. I let go of her hair. "On the bed." She scrambles to get on quickly, awkwardly going on her knees and hands. I breathe for a moment to calm my anger. "I had to repeat an order to you again, girl. Do you think that should go unpunished?"

"...No, Sir..." Her voice is shaking and she's hiding under her hair again, head down.

"You've been a bad girl. Ask me nicely to make you my good girl again." I can see her body shake more. I smile. I like humiliating her. Forcing her to participate in her own punishment. *She'll learn to beg me for what she needs.*

"Please..." I wait to see if she'll say more. I sigh deeply when she doesn't.

"No. Full sentences, Lucy. You'll ask in a strong voice for exactly what you deserve. Now."

She turns her head and looks at me standing behind her. Even through her hair, I can see she's turning red again and pleading with her eyes. I wait. This time I can be patient with her. In the future, I'll expect quicker responses. *But we'll get there.*

70 Her

I try to think, but my mind goes blank at his words. My arms and back still sting and tingle, little spots of fire feeding the need of my pussy. *He called me a pain slut. I am.* I never realized how much until now. Until he started torturing every inch of me with his little slaps, hardly touching me except with his belt. I eagerly waited for each strike, like an itch I didn't know I had, but desperately need scratched.

But this? I can't do this. I can't stay here like a dog and beg for him to hurt me more. I lower my head again, trying to breathe. *Maybe if I wait, he'll just get angry enough to beat me. I won't have to say anything except that I'm sorry.* He's in my head though, "We can wait here like this all night, beautiful, if that's what it takes."

I look at him again. He only looks a little angry. I'm shaken by this. I feel the tears drop to the bed when I lower my head again. Max always hurt me when he was angry. He'd punish me based on how angry I had made him. He was rough during sex most of the time, but he never used the belt unless he was angry.

Seeing Jake so calm... I shake harder. "Why are you doing this?" I didn't mean to say it out loud, but I can't help myself. I can hear the tears in my voice and I don't try to stop them. I let out a soft sob with a shaky breath.

I feel him move closer to the bed, but he still doesn't touch me. "You need to learn this lesson, Lucy." I feel him move back a little. Turning my head slightly, I can see him unwrap the belt from his hand, letting the leather hang down. I turn my face away. *Good. I won't have to say anything.* "Arch your back, put your ass in the air for me." I do, eager to please him, eager for him to start, scared and excited. *It's been too long...*

But he doesn't hit me. "The lesson you need to learn, girl. What is it?"

I open and close my mouth a few times. This is torture. Exposed like this, knowing he's staring at me. Knowing that he knows that I'm just waiting for him to spank me, that I'll stay in this position until he does. *Well, no.*

I push myself up, onto my knees, turning to look at him, arms crossed over my chest. "Why don't you just tell me what it is you want, Jake?"

And he smiles. *Damn him*! He even laughs a little. "Are you trying to make me angry, Lucy? Is that what you think will work here?" But it does work, his face changes quickly to his stern stony glare and he steps closer to me. I lose my nerve and drop my arms to my sides, but stay on my knees, meeting his eyes at least.

"I know what you're used to, girl. I know what's going on in your little girl head." He grabs me by my hair again, yanking even harder and pulling me off balance. "You think the only way you can submit to me is if you make me angry?" His pull on my head is causing my eyes to water and I'm gasping, but I stop myself from trying to pull away from him. He shakes me with each word again, rattling my teeth, "You think the only way I'm going to demand your obedience is with anger?" He lets go of my head and shoves me away. I fall back down onto my hands and he barks the order, "Stay."

I do. I'm shaken and frightened. I have no idea what he'll do. Jake's confused everything, my head and body shouting to run, to stay. I blink my tears, sniffling, hiding behind my hair again. My head throbs from his touch.

I can hear him breathing heavily behind me. When he speaks, his voice is controlled, even, darkly edged. "The lesson you need to learn is that I'm not Max." I shoot him a hard look. *How dare he bring up Max now, when I'm like this!* I start to sit up again, but stop at the cold, calmness of his voice. "If you move again, girl, I will *tie* you to that bed."

I relax back onto my hands slowly. When he continues, I can hear the need in him. Anger mixed with passion and longing. It mirrors my own. "Your heart belonged to him first…maybe always will. I know I can only hope for a small piece to belong to me. But that's enough. Loving you, like this; having you, like this…it's enough for me."

"You love me?" My voice is tiny, I don't want him to hear my own need. I don't want to admit how desperate I am for him.

"Yes. With *all* of *my* heart, Lucy." But it's a cold, calm response. I resist turning to see his face.

"....But you don't want *all* of mine?"

"I didn't say that. I said I know that Max will always be a part of you." He moves towards me again, reaching with his hand under me, shocking me by his warmth and gentle touch. "This baby will always have a part of you too. But this part," he moves his hand down between my legs and I push towards his fingers, moaning before I can stop myself. "I won't share. This part belongs to me now. I won't have you thinking of him when I touch you. I won't have you thinking of him when I'm inside you. I won't have you thinking of him when you're with me ever again." I moan at the deep pressing of his fingers. "You *are* mine now, Lucy. I'll let you keep a part to yourself...but the rest...you belong to *me*."

I nod, my hair whipping the sheets. I turn my head and smile a little, "I do belong to you now. And I love you, too." I moan at the release of his hand. He steps back again.

"Then show me what a good girl you want to be for me. Ask for what you know you deserve."

I swallow and breathe for a moment. I push thoughts of Max out of my head and concentrate instead on my fingers on the bed, on the feel of the sheets under me, on Jake's breathing near me. I raise my head a little, but close my eyes. My voice is extra high and small, "I...I deserve a spanking. Please?"

And he laughs at me! I turn my head to see him smiling and shaking his head. "That's not the best you can do, girl. Try again. Start with why you deserve to be punished."

I have to swallow the anger I felt at his laughter for a moment, but it makes my voice a little stronger. "I didn't obey your order, so I deserve to be spanked. Sir!" It's a petulant response. He just brings this out in me. Especially since he's laughing at me again.

"And now you can add being bratty to your list of reasons. I'll give you one more chance to get this right." His voice lowers even more, sending chills down my spine, "Get it wrong this time and I'll get out a thicker belt to use."

I swallow at this thought. *I don't think Jake would ever hurt me as much as...* I stop myself. I swallow again. "I'm sorry." I have to breathe a little more to get over the need to cry again. I know he doesn't want that. *And I know he's right. I have to decide for myself. To be here, to be with him, like this. I love him. I've known this for a while. And loving him means I have to let go...I have to be free of the hold Max has on me...*

I have a clear mental image of myself right now. The humiliating position, the lack of any place to hide, the openness to Jake physically. I trust him enough to be here like this. I take a deep breath and picture a collar on my neck, with a chain attached. I mentally place the chain in Jake's hands. I smile a little. *Not that I want* that *exactly...well...maybe...*

I try for a calm, clear voice, my smile still evident, "I...I hesitated following your orders...and I've been disrespectful."

He sighs, "Good girl."

I turn my head back and wipe my hair away from my face quickly to see him clearly. He's smiling at me. A sweet, full smile. The kind I know I will long for every day of my life. The kind I know I will have with him every day too. I know I'll do anything to please him, to earn his smiles, to feel this again.

I'm sore and my arms are getting tired. My eyes burn with tears and I'm afraid of what he'll do to me. But I want more. I want him, more from him. I need this from him. I want to give myself to him…*the only way I know how…completely.*

"I need to please you, Jake. Please punish me…make me yours completely…"

71 Him

I flick the belt in my hand, feeling the light weight. With her eyes still watching me, I smile and give her the first real whip with the belt. I like the sound, the crack, her ass wiggles and moves for me. Her cry catches in her throat. And most important. I can see the clear red line across her cheeks form.

I'm not going to be able to ignore my hard cock for long now.

I crack the belt against her cheeks again in almost the same spot, where her ass meets her legs. Her cry is louder. "I said be quiet, girl. If you can't hold your cry, then tell me you need to be gagged." I smile at this thought, picturing her mouth stretched open.

She whimpers and shakes her head, "No, Sir…please!"

Damn. She makes it hard to keep going. But that only makes me hit her harder, same spot. She holds her breath, pushing it out with a loud pop and long hiss. I don't give her a moment to hold it again. *I'm a bastard, I want to torture her, to force her to cry out and beg.*

I hit her again, same spot and love watching her move this time. Her knees shake and pump against the bed. Her cry is louder, but snatched back quickly. *Good girl. Let's see if you can do that again.*

Same spot, same speed, more deep redness. She'll have a welt there for sure. Her legs only shake this time, her arms too. Her cry is a long slow whimper. Her head hanging down.

I step forward and rub her ass. She moves her cheeks away quickly like my touch stings as much as the belt. *It probably does.* I pinch the redness and she yelps. But she stays put. She even arches her ass for me. "Good girl."

I wrap the belt back around my hand. "Stay exactly as you are. No sound. No movement. I won't make this easy, but I will make it fast, beautiful. I need to be inside you." She moans for me.

I start back up with the small slaps of the belt, wrapping its end around each leg at a time, taking extra care to hit the tender part of her inner thighs. I enjoy her quick intake of breath, her head whipping back in pain each time.

But she stays put, she only breathes and hisses through each strike. When I get to her feet, I stop and kiss each sole. She squirms. I bring the belt down harder and she almost cries out in shock, just stopping herself from forming any words or getting louder. *Good girl.* I only give her a second to pant against this pain.

"Spread your legs." She moves to open her knees quickly. I smile. *She thinks she's done.*

I move slowly to stand next to her, rubbing the part of her ass that's only a little pink. I whisper, "There's only one more spot I need to claim with my belt, Lucy." I can feel her shaking increase as she takes my meaning. "Stay still!" I keep my hand on her ass to help her not to move.

I rub the tip of the belt against her wet lips. I can see the leather darken with it. I pull the belt back and hear her take a quick breath in, holding it. I wait a little longer, enjoying her anticipation. I bring the belt down hard against her pussy and asshole, a wet smack and sharp cry. She's almost hyperventilating from it.

I cut into her breathing, "Get control of yourself, girl. I'll give you another if you keep crying and breathing like that."

But I smile that she doesn't close her legs. She lowers her head and takes deeper breaths. I move away from the bed, dropping the belt and getting undressed quickly.

I'm on the bed, behind her just as her breathing is almost back to normal. I squeeze her lower ass, the welt mark, and she hisses again. I move my thumbs to her pussy lips, feeling the swelling and wetness. *She'll be sore. Just the way I like her.*

I pull her lips apart roughly and she's gasping already, pushing towards me. I lean over and run my tongue up and down the inside of her pussy, sucking her juices and scraping her swollen lips with my teeth. She cries out again, but still pushes into me more, arching more. *So beautiful.*

I pull back and hear her little moans. Watch her ass pump up and down a little for me. *God help me if I can make it more than 30 seconds, but I'll try, girl.*

I push my cock slowly into her, feeling her tight, wet pussy wrap around me, feeling her lips pull and squeeze me deeper. She can take all of me. I can feel her wall, but she takes it, even pushing herself further onto me, crying out.

I pull back and shove in hard, slapping my balls against her clit. We cry out together, grunt together. I push in harder once before pulling out quick and shoving back in quicker. She matches my moves, shoving and pulling, squeezing when I'm deepest. I only hold on long enough to hear the start of her long moan.

My own cry drowns hers. My fingers cut into her hips, pulling and shoving her on my cock. She falls to her elbows, crying and moaning. I wait until my cock stops throbbing, until her hips stop moving at all, before pulling out and pushing her sideways.

I collapse next to her and grab her in my arms. "I love you…I love you…I love you!" I kiss her lips, taking her breath to make it my own.

She laughs and slaps my chest. "Give a girl a minute, you brute!" But she quickly pulls herself onto my chest, smothering me with her kisses and hair. "I love you, too."

…..

"I want to show you something." I get up and pull her with me. We walk naked through my loft, hand in hand.

I open the door down the hall and reach for the light switch inside, letting her walk in first.

"When did you do all this?" She's beautiful, with her hand on her stomach, hair falling around her shoulders, my belt marks pinking her skin in lines across her legs, arms, and back. Her ass is a beautiful cherry red as she walks into the nursery.

It's all set up for her. There's a comfy rocker, furniture, tons of toys and books, everything she could want.

"Today. I had my contractors here all day getting it together." She turns and sees my smile and the wall behind me.

She frowns, but I only smile more. She walks over and stands in front of the art, "MJT," hand painted with tiny cartoon animals joined together inside the initials. I stand behind her and put my hands over hers, still on her stomach. I can feel her warmth.

I see goose bumps run down her stinging arms with my voice against her ear, "Our son will be named Maximilian Jacob Traeger when he's born." I turn her around in my arms, she smiles at me with tears. "MJ for short I'm thinking."

72 Her

"And what if I'd said no to being yours?" I tease him with a coy smile and kiss on his chin.

He only laughs. And swats my ass hard. I cry out. "Are you asking for another spanking so soon, girl?" I shake my head. He turns a little more serious. "I know you didn't have a choice." He kisses me and I'm filled again with the complete passion of his touch. Even with only a small kiss, every part of me is claimed as his. I feel it down to my toes. I feel everywhere that he touched with his belt, his lips. "I want you to move in here, Lucy. I don't have a ring; I'll take care of that tomorrow, but I want to make you my wife. Say yes."

I put my arms around his neck. "Two weeks."

"What?" I laugh at his confusion and stern frown. I kiss him quickly.

"We'll get married in two weeks, on Saturday and I'll move in then." I step away from his arms and walk back out into the hall. I know his eyes are on my ass, on the marks he's left on me. I smile. "That should give you enough time to get this place ready for a nice party to celebrate." He comes up behind me laughing and picking me up, spinning me around and heading back into the bedroom. *I can picture a future again. With Jake. Here.*

I allow myself one more thought before giving into his kisses, the tiny part I know Jake will always let me have…

I can picture a future with our baby very loved, Max…and he will know you through Jake and me. You will always have a piece of my heart. Always.

In the dark, listening to Jake's little snores, I know he's right. I know I'm his now. I know he's mine. My heart may never heal completely from losing Max and I'd never forgive myself if I let go of the love I still have for him. But I know Jake loves me. And I love him. He's given me everything I want, everything I need…him.

Control is about choices. And I didn't have any before.

I didn't choose to let fate step in my way. It just did.

I didn't choose to fall for him. I just did.

I didn't choose to give him everything I am. I just had to.

I have no choice in how I love him. I just do.

I can be strong. I can submit all of myself again. And he just accepts me as I am.

Always.

The **alternate** ending for Max and Lucy can be read in

True Control 4.1.